D0722692

3 1232 00159 5026

Yellowthread Street

Also by William Marshall

THE FIRE CIRCLE
THE AGE OF DEATH
THE MIDDLE KINGDOM

A RINEHART SUSPENSE NOVEL

Yellowthread Street

WILLIAM MARSHALL

HOLT, RINEHART AND WINSTON
New York

Library of Congress Cataloging in Publication Data
Marshall, William Leonard,
Yellowthread Street.

(A Rinehart suspense novel)
I. Title.
PZ4.M372Ye [PR9619.3.M275] 823 75-29721
ISBN 0-03-016836-8

First published in the United States in 1976

Printed in the United States of America

10 9 8 7 6 5 4 3 2 1

for Gerald and Elvire

The Hong Bay district of Hong Kong is fictitious, as are the people who, for one reason or another, inhabit it.

Hong Kong invites, entices, accepts, accommodates, pleasures, puts up with, cheats and disgorges several dozen million tourists a year, and almost without exception they all leave their air-conditioned, room-serviced, overpriced glass and concrete hotel cocoons with the delicious feeling that, just below the surface of this bursting town, just around the corner from where they bought their transistor radio or made a good deal on their brand-new stereo equipment, there are sinister, secret and very seedy happenings going on.

Most of them keep away from Hong Bay and the bar and dance-hall district around Yellowthread Street (the brochures the Tourist Office hands out say you should) which is where the secret and seedy happenings happen and they go home safe with slides and eight millimetre home movies proving they had a wonderful time.

P.M.

As Detective Inspector Phil Auden went through the door of the Yellowthread Street Police Station in the district of Hong Bay and the day shift left, night fell, seven Jumbo jets carrying a total of two thousand tourists, businessmen, wives and others landed in procession at Kai Tak airport, an American destroyer disembarked eight hundred bored, thirsty, lustful, belligerent sailors for forty-eight hours shore leave, and the Chinese Communists across the border took it into their heads to turn the water off.

Constable Sun looked up from his desk and said, 'They've turned the water off.'

'Shit!' said Detective Inspector Auden.

Four streets away from the Yellowthread Street Police Station where Detective Inspector Auden said 'Shit!' and Constable Sun shrugged, a man named Chen went back to his room in Cuttlefish Lane near the fish markets with an axe and used it to halve his wife and quarter her boyfriend.

Bill Spencer said, 'When was that?'

'Just now,' Constable Sun said, 'my brother rang me to ask if I could get him some.'

'How are you supposed to be able to get him water?' Auden asked.

Sun shrugged.

'Hey,' Spencer said to Auden, 'Inspector Feiffer left a message he got a tip on the rickshaw basher. He's gone down to the harbour.'

'Does he want me?'

'No.' Spencer leaned forward on the report typewriter and contemplated the spelling mistakes that were the fault of the machine.

'How are you supposed to be the water man?' Auden asked Sun.

Sun went inscrutable. 'Don't go inscrutable,' Auden said.

'My brother's a nut,' Constable Sun said. He looked over at one of the uniformed men, another Hakka-speaking harbour inhabitant named Cho, 'Isn't he?'

'His brother's crazy,' Cho said. He was considering the angle of his cap in the dusty glass of the portrait of the Queen. He said, 'I've known him for years. He's always been crazy.' He settled his cap.

'Hmm,' Auden said. He went to his desk and sat down.

Eight of them and the cleaner named Ah Pin made up the nightshift: Auden, Spencer, Sun, Cho, another uniformed Constable named Lee, Harry Feiffer who was a full Detective Chief Inspector, and Christopher O'Yee who claimed he had an Irish father and a Shanghai mother (or the other way around). Feiffer and O'Yee came through the door together.

Spencer watched Feiffer come in. Feiffer was a big man with tired eyes. He wore a white suit that had been white when it had been made in Hanford Road but had got darker and more faded and stained the longer he wore it in Yellowthread Street. O'Yee came in, went to his desk, took off his coat and shoulder holster, and sat down to get comfortable as the phone rang.

'Did you get him?' Spencer asked Feiffer, '—the rickshaw man?'

'No.'

O'Yee said, 'Yellowthread Street Police Station,' into the telephone. It was a gamble every time it rang. If it was a Chinese speaker bursting to report a violation of the peace or blood running down a tenement wall on to his produce or into his customers' soup it took a few seconds for each of them to get their ears and voices set to Cantonese and by that time the hysterical citizen might have decided he was talking to an English laundry and hung up.

This time it was an English voice and it said, 'The *Scranton*'s back.'

'Who's this?'

'Harbourmaster,' the voice said. 'Who's this?'

'Detective Inspector O'Yee.'

'Where's Inspector Feiffer?'

'He's here.'

'Tell him the *Scranton*'s back,' the voice said, 'I'm very busy,' and hung up.

O'Yee looked over at Harry Feiffer. Feiffer was going through his desk for a blank report form and swearing.

'The *Scranton*'s back,' O'Yee said.

'Oh ho,' Feiffer said enthusiastically and shut the desk. He seemed very pleased about something. He said, 'You like movies, don't you?'

'I like what?' O'Yee said. But just then Feiffer's phone rang and this time it was an hysterical Chinese, a lady, reporting that blood was running down the stairs in her rooming establishment in Cuttlefish Lane and Feiffer took Sun with him and left before O'Yee found out who or what the *Scranton* was and why, if he did, he should like the movies.

He said to Auden, 'This is a hell of a life,' and Auden, who hardly ever knew what an Irish Chinaman or a Chinese Mick with an American accent was talking about anyway, nodded automatically.

The hysterical lady's name was Mrs Fan and she was a fat hysterical lady standing on the portal to her rickety wooden unpainted smelly establishment holding her temples in with her hands and screaming for the police.

'We're the police,' Feiffer said. He pointed at Sun's uniform to prove the point.

Mrs Fan went on screaming.

Feiffer and Sun went up the stairs.

The bodies were in a room on the third floor at the end of the corridor, on the bed. Whoever had found them had taken one look, left the door open, and run shouting towards the stairs. Along the corridor there were bloody footprints and a skidding smudge where the finder had lost his balance in his haste to get away.

'The woman,' Constable Sun said, 'I noticed her shoes.'

Feiffer nodded. He went into the room and wondered where they drained away the blood from the cuts of meat in butchers' shops. A light was on in the room and it turned the blood into an off-red colour and made it glisten like women's lacquered hair under neon light. A pile of bloody clothing was in one corner of the room and the plywood screen to a makeshift cupboard had been thrown on to the floor beside it. A few of the plywood sections had blood on them and there were bloody handprints on a towel on top of it.

Feiffer went over to the pile of clothing and moved the pieces apart with his finger. There were underpants, socks, a shirt, trousers, and a handkerchief.

'He lives here,' Feiffer said. Both the bodies were naked. Feiffer pointed to the dead man, 'He thought he did too, on and off.' He glanced at the clothing again. 'He even took a clean handkerchief and left the old one for her to wash.'

Sun looked like he thought that was a poor joke.

'Force of habit,' Feiffer said.

'The husband?'

'Go through the other clothes in the cupboard. Some of them are probably the boyfriend's. And call the Medical Examiner when you're done.'

'There's the axe,' Sun said. It lay behind the door. It didn't look very sharp, but it must have been to have made such neat cuts.

Feiffer went to the dressing table. It was just to one side of the bed and blood lay like snail tracks across its surface. He took up a framed photograph showing two men and a woman looking proud and hopeful in front of a street food stall somewhere between Cat Street and Beach Road. Between two buildings you could almost see the harbour.

'Is this him?'

Sun looked over at the photograph.

'Now look at the body.'

Sun looked. 'It's him. And her.'

'And the other one's the husband,' Feiffer said. He looked at the inscription above the stall in the photograph and tried to make out the minute identity licence tacked to its wooden supports. The licence card was too small, but the characters said 'Chen and Wang'. He said to Sun, 'The dead one's probably Wang. Chen's wearing a wedding ring.'

'So—' Sun said. He kept trying to find somewhere else to look apart from the bed. Mrs Fan came heavily up the stairs. She had changed her steady hysterical screaming into steady hysterical screaming and Sun was glad to turn his attention to her.

'Find out from her who's who,' Feiffer said, 'and get the doctor, fingerprints and the photographer up.'

'Where are you going?'

'I'm going to the food stall to arrest the other one.'

'He won't have gone to work after this,' Sun said.

Feiffer nodded at the soiled handkerchief on top of the pile of bloody clothes. 'Force of habit,' he said and went out to leave Mrs Fan and the screaming to Sun.

'Who's this?' the voice on the other end of the phone demanded.

O'Yee said, 'This is Detective Inspector Christopher O'Yee, who the bloody hell is this?'

'The *Scranton*'s back,' the voice said.

'I'm getting sick of this.'

'Is Inspector Feiffer there?'

'No.'

'Oh. Tell him the—'

'You're not the Harbourmaster,' O'Yee said.

'What?'

'The Harbourmaster.'

'Of course not!'

'Who are you?'

'Inspector Feiffer said one of his men would come down here while it's in. We're next. He said we'd be next and now it's in again. He made a promise to me.'

'You're next?'

'Yes!'

'Next for what?'

The voice obviously thought he was slow. 'For the *Scranton*,' the voice said. 'You're slow. Who is this?'

'I'm a policeman,' O'Yee said. 'What or who is the *Scranton*?'

'The *Scranton* is an American destroyer of course!'

'Of course it is,' O'Yee said. 'Now who are you?' He waited.

'This is the manager of the Peacock Cinema on Icehouse Street of course!'

'Of course it is,' O'Yee said. 'Now what can I do for you?' He thought he sounded very civil for a man fast going paranoid. 'What seems to be your problem?'

'Didn't Inspector Feiffer tell you?'

'No.' He said, 'Did you say *Cinema*?' Something went 'click' in his mind.

'The Peacock on—'

'I think I'm your man,' O'Yee said. 'Why don't you take it slowly for me?'

At the other end of the line he heard the man sigh and draw a calming breath before he began to take it slowly for him.

Minnie Oh was a clerical error. Someone in Police Administration in Salisbury Road had decided Yellowthread Street needed a woman police constable with a hard face and an unsympathetic manner for the whores and madames off Icehouse Street and the Jasmine Steps, and by mistake they sent Minnie.

She had even been given an office at the rear of the station.

Both Auden and Spencer had an overwhelming urge for Minnie, not to mention the urges of Constable Lee, Constable Sun and the eighty-year-old cleaner Ah Pin, and so when the American woman from New Jersey (she said, 'I'm from New Jersey') came in wearing a camera she had purchased at the airport (it still had the shop label on it) and a voluminous raffia bag for the things she was going to purchase and said, 'I've lost my husband,' Spencer thought it was an ideal opportunity to steal a quick march on the opposition.

He said, 'Best if you see the Woman Police Officer.'

The New Jersey lady looked around the room. The desks were all scarred, untidy and inefficient looking and the two tone paint on the walls—green and faded green—reminded her of precinct stations in New Jersey, so she knew she wasn't going to get any satisfaction anyway. She said, 'I don't care who I see.'

'Matters of a personal nature—' Spencer said. He glanced towards the corridor that led to Minnie's room.

'It's not that personal.'

'Well—' Spencer said.

'We were walking along and I lost him.'

'I see.'

'Yeah.' She looked at the room and looked like she did not approve. 'I thought you British cops did better than this.'

'I don't know,' Spencer said, 'I've only been here two weeks.' He said, 'I was with Administration.' She couldn't have cared less. He said, 'I've just passed my detective's exam.' Spencer said, 'Will I get you the Woman Police Officer?'

'O.K.' the New Jersey lady said.

'Name?'

'I don't know anybody. We just got off the plane. Goddamned airline lost the baggage so we've been wandering around waiting for it to turn up. I haven't even got a hotel—'

'No,' Spencer said, 'Your name?'

'Skilbeck.'

'I'll get the W.P.C.' He went down the corridor and tapped lightly on the door with a tingle of anticipation. He thought of Minnie's face on a white pillow with her black hair and brown eyes and— He thought, 'Say, "Hullo, Bill"—'

Minnie came out.

'Minnie,' Spencer said.

Minnie said, 'Hullo, Bill.'

'How long's he going to be?' Mrs Skilbeck asked O'Yee.

The cinema manager's voice said, 'The U.S.S. *Scranton*—'

'I've got that.'

'Hey,' the American lady said.

'Yes?' O'Yee said.

'The last time it was in—'

'Just a minute.'

'How long's he going to be?'

'Who?'

'The one with the yellow hair.'

'Inspector Spencer?'

'If you say so.'

'What's the matter?' the manager asked, 'am I going too fast for you again?'

'Wait a minute. He'll be back in a moment. Excuse me.' He said to the manager, 'The U.S.S. *Scranton*—'

'Weren't you here last year when we had the—'

'No.'

'You don't remember the cinema robberies?'

'No.'

The manager drew a calming breath. He had had nothing but the cinema robberies on his mind for over thirteen months and it annoyed him that the full weight of the forces of law and order had had other things to think about.

'Well?'

'Well?'

'Well, tell me.'

The manager sighed. The manager said, 'I'll explain it to you.'

The manager explained between more sighs. The manager explained that thirteen months ago, over a period of forty-eight hours, there had been three hold-ups of cinema cashiers and that an amount veering close to the sort of figures you only heard at bankruptcy hearings had been taken. It was a Negro gunman in a sailor suit and the *Scranton* had been the only American ship in port at the time and they had had forty-eight hours shore leave.

'Jesus!' the American lady said, and Auden, who also thought Spencer was taking too long with Minnie for a simple matter of police business, said, 'He's been gone a long time.'

'He had a gun,' the cinema manager said. 'Inspector Feiffer said—'

'I'll get him for you,' Auden said.

'What did he say?'

'He said he'd have one of his men take over the cashier's job when the *Scranton* came back.'

'If he was from the *Scranton* why wasn't he arrested the last time it was in? Don't tell me all Negroes look the same.'

There was a silence at the other end of the line. Auden poked his head around the corridor and called, 'Inspector Spencer—'

'Well?' O'Yee said.

There was silence at the other end of the line in the manager's office of the Peacock Cinema on Icehouse Street. O'Yee thought, 'He is going to tell me all Negroes look the same.' 'O.K.,' O'Yee said, 'I guess I'm the man for the job.'

'Inspector Feiffer said it would have to be a Chinese policeman.'

'I'm Eurasian,' O'Yee said.

Spencer came back down the corridor with Minnie Oh. He looked pleased with himself. Auden said irritably, 'This lady's been waiting.'

'All right,' the cinema manager said. His voice had the

resignation of a man who thought he was going to be robbed and the police were going to assist the robber to get away with it. He said lamely, 'The *Scranton* came in this evening.'

'So I've gathered. I'll come down. You're open all evening?'

'All evening and all night.' The manager said, 'He's got a gun.'

'So have I.'

Minnie said, 'How can I help you?'

'Didn't he tell you? My husband's missing. For Chrissakes!'

'He said "lost".'

'O.K. "lost". I went into a store to get something of a personal female nature and when I came out he was gone. "Lost." "Missing."—gone.'

Minnie took out an incident sheet for the details. Auden and Spencer went back to their desks out of earshot.

'You'll have to do.' The manager said, 'I'll wait for you outside,' and hung up.

Minnie told the New Jersey lady that her husband would turn up and that she should come back in an hour to see if he had. She said, 'That's the best we can do. He's probably gone into a bar for a drink.'

'He had better not,' Mrs Skilbeck said. She thought the place looked just like the precinct stations in New Jersey. She shook her head in pessimistic disgust and went out.

O'Yee decided he was not going to sit there and check his gun. He thought it was the sort of thing cops only did in old movies. He thought if he had forgotten to load the damn thing then he deserved to get shot and there was no point in checking it anyway. He said to Auden, 'What's the movie at the Peacock?'

'What?' Auden said. He was watching Minnie's long legs. 'That John Wayne film—the one where he's got a machine gun that shoots thirty bullets a second. *McQ* or *O Yez* or something. I don't remember. All the cops get killed in it.'

'I've seen it,' O'Yee said, and checked his gun.

'Licensing Department.' It was a Hong Kong university

educated Chinese voice speaking English, 'Night Duty Clerk.'

Feiffer was ringing from a leather goods and luggage shop. He cupped his hand around the mouthpiece of the telephone to keep his business private. 'This is Detective Chief Inspector Feiffer of the Yellowthread Street Police Station.'

'I beg your pardon?'

'Feiffer.'

'Did you say you were the police?'

'That's right. I want some information about the location of a certain food stall somewhere between Cat Street and Beach Road, Hong Bay.'

'Your voice sounds muffled.'

'I'm ringing from a luggage shop. I don't want them to hear.'

'You said you were the police. Is this some sort of joke? Is that you, George?'

'This is Detective Chief Inspector Harry Feiffer of the—'

'I think I'd better ring the police station.'

'I'm not ringing from the police station. I'm ringing from a luggage shop because it was the only phone I could find that wasn't being used. I want some information.'

'What sort of information?'

'I want the exact location of a food stall in the Hong Bay area.'

'I don't know. Are you sure this isn't—'

'Are you the person to speak to?'

'Oh, yes.'

'In that case the name of the stall is Chen and Wang. It's a street food stall. It's somewhere in the Cat Street area near the Bay. I'm in that area now, but half of the stalls are still closed and they don't have their signs out.'

'What time is it?'

'It's eight o'clock.'

'Most of them don't open until nine. I often go to a street stall for a meal myself, although I must say, not in the Hong Bay district. It isn't safe.'

'I'm trying to make it safe. I'm a policeman. Now can you just give me the information?'

'I'm not sure about this. I'd better have your full name and rank. I'll write it down.' That would make it all right.

'My full name is Harry Feiffer and I'm a Detective Chief Inspector at Yellowthread Street Police Station in the district of Hong Bay on Her Majesty's Crown Colony of bloody Hong Kong and can I please have the information?'

'How do you spell that?'

'I-n-f-o-r—'

'Feiffer.'

'F-e-i-f-f-e-r-fullstop. I'm in a hurry.'

'I assume this is a serious crime you're investigating?'

'None of your damn business. Have you got the information or not?'

'Oh, yes,' the voice said, 'I've got the card index in front of me by a funny coincidence. I was just looking over an application for a new shoe stall and the girl made a mistake and brought me all the—'

'Chen and Wang,' Feiffer said. 'Street stall, food, location of.' The proprietor of the luggage shop kept glancing at him and blinking at the hand cupped over the mouthpiece. 'He thinks I'm a kidnapper,' Feiffer thought. The proprietor thought he was an extortionist.

'Wait a minute,' the Night Duty Clerk said.

Feiffer waited. He grinned reassuringly at the proprietor. The proprietor looked away.

'No,' the Night Duty Clerk said.

'What do you mean, "no"?'

'There isn't any such stall. Are you sure you got the name right?'

'Yes.'

'Then no.'

'Then no, what?'

'Then, no, it doesn't exist. You probably got the name wrong.'

'I got the name right.'

There was a pause at the other end of the line. 'Really? I thought we'd closed all the unlicensed stalls. I'll put you on to our investigation section.'

'I don't want to talk to your—'

'They're policemen there too,' the Night Duty Clerk said soothingly, 'You can—'—he broke off—'I'm astounded there's still one in that area we missed. It is very serious. I'll transfer you.'

Feiffer hung up. The luggage shop proprietor breathed a sigh of relief.

'My mother,' Feiffer said. The proprietor nodded and kept one eye on his cashbox. 'Deaf,' Feiffer said and tapped at his ear. The proprietor stared at the bulge Feiffer's pistol made under his coat.

'Policeman,' Feiffer said and tapped at his coat bulge and that seemed the most unlikely tap of all.

Hong Kong itself is an island of some 30 square miles under British administration in the South China Sea facing the Kowloon and New Territories areas of continental China. Kowloon and the New Territories are also British administered, surrounded by the Communist Chinese province of Kwantung. The climate is generally sub-tropical with hot, humid summers and heavy rainfall. The population of Hong Kong and the surrounding areas at any one time, including tourists and visitors, is in excess of four millions. The New Territories are leased from the Chinese. The lease is due to expire in 1997 but the British nevertheless maintain a military presence along the border although, should they ever desire to terminate the lease early, the Communists, who supply all the Colony's water, need only turn off the taps. Hong Bay is on the southern side of the island and the tourist brochures advise you not to go there after dark.

The woodcarvers used to be in Camphorwood Lane and the

smaller goldsmiths used to be situated one after the other in the Jasmine Steps area and Goldsmiths' Street used to be where you could find undertakers. The undertakers moved away to the Street of Undertakers and the larger goldsmiths moved into Goldsmiths' Street. The woodcarvers then moved en masse into Wyang Street and evicted several hordes of tailors. The tailors moved into Hanford Road and evicted the ivory carvers. That left Camphorwood Street empty and several posses of ivory carvers premises-less. The smaller goldsmiths moved into Camphorwood Lane and the ivory carvers went around to the Jasmine Steps. The Jasmine Steps already had new tenants. The African governments decided no more elephants were going to be shot for ivory so the ivory carvers became small goldsmiths and moved into Camphorwood Lane with the smaller goldsmiths. So when the Mongolian decided to move his business to Camphorwood Lane he had plenty of customers to choose from.

The Mongolian went to the first small goldsmith's at the west end of Camphorwood Lane off Canton Street (you are not expected to remember any of this) and asked to see the owner.

It was just after eight o'clock and he was the only customer. At Camphorwood Lane at that time of night there was probably only one customer in each of the thirty or forty smaller goldsmiths' shops so things were very slow for Hong Bay. In Cartier's or Tiffany's it probably would have amounted to a riot.

The Mongolian was well over six feet three inches tall and he weighed in at two hundred and eighty-five pounds even with a shaved head and he wore three signet rings on his right hand and four on his left hand. Each of the rings was made out of brass and since they were not joined together they were technically not brass knuckles, although Mr Yin, who owned the first smaller goldsmith's shop, wasn't so sure.

'A hundred dollars,' the Mongolian said and drew an Indian Gurkha kukri knife with an eleven-inch blade and a silver lion's head pommel from under his shirt.

Mr Yin cocked his head to suggest he had not heard correctly so the Mongolian grabbed him by the wrist, laid his fingers flat on the glass display table, held the kukri a few inches above it and said again, 'A hundred dollars.'

At twenty-five dollars a finger Mr Yin did not think the price exorbitant, and if he calculated it—he did, swiftly—at eight dollars fifty a joint, it was downright reasonable.

Mr Yin paid.

The Mongolian grunted and went next door.

Next door, Mr Kwan calculated it at thirty dollars a pint of blood and thought it was the bargain of the year.

In the shop next to that, Mr Ho, who had a mind quicker and more logical than either of his two previous colleagues, made the equation at twenty-five dollars for his mistress, two dollars fifty each for his two wives, fifteen for his aged father and five dollars for each of his eleven children and retrieved his hand considering himself a man of decision.

The Mongolian sheathed his kukri, said, 'I'll be back again,' and watched Mr Ho nod happily. Mr Ho raised his other hand and even waved a little. Mr Ho's assistant watched the Mongolian leave and then reached for the phone. It was a pleasure, Mr Ho thought, an absolute pleasure to be able to put two complete hands on the instrument to stop him.

His assistant said, 'Police—'

Mr Ho looked horrified and waved his index finger at him again. He looked at the index finger and the other fingers surrounding it and thought they made a nice set.

'He wouldn't have done it,' Mr Ho's assistant said. His face said he thought Mr Ho weak, contemptible and cowardly. He was Mr Ho's nephew whom Mr Ho hadn't taken into his finger calculations anyway so Mr Ho fired him.

The Mongolian went next door and repeated his transaction with Mr Yin. By now, he was four hundred dollars the richer. He went next door to *Alice's Goldsmith's and Jewellery* and made his first mistake.

For those who take the Tourist Office's advice and stay away from Hong Bay it will come as news to hear that there are bad ladies in the night area between Beach Road where it circles along the shantytown area and the Jasmine Steps where the ex-ivory carvers sit about complaining about Jomo Kenyatta and General Amin. There are also bad men who have a financial interest in the bad ladies, but they live high up on Hanford Hill in villas in the next district so they leave the administration of the bad ladies to older badder ladies like Hot Time Alice Ping and you hardly ever see the bad men.

Now Hot Time Alice Ping had been an older badder lady for some twenty years and in that time she had learned that human flesh is a fragile thing and liable to rust and deterioration and she had put some of her money into other things. One of them was *Alice's Goldsmith's and Jewellery*, and she was very happy about the steady, respectable profit it returned. And because she was happy the men on Hanford Hill who you hardly ever saw were happy, and because they were happy and you hardly ever saw them and they did their thuggery and killings somewhere else the Yellowthread Street police were generally happy.

So when the Mongolian, a freelance operator, decided that Alice, and in turn the men on the hill and in turn the police, could spare a hundred dollars every so often or wouldn't object to their manager who made them a steady profit having his hand left on the glass counter while he went away to do something else like bleed to death, he set in motion a number of events which led to everyone being so sure he weighed in at two hundred and eighty-five pounds exactly even with his shaven head.

The Mortuary people are very precise about such things.

The first reaction the manager of Alice's little enterprise had when the Mongolian suspended the kukri above his right tentacle was to smile knowingly at him and say, 'Piss off.'

The Mongolian, feeling his winning streak might well desert him if he was to let this go unchallenged, hit him in the face with his left hand collection of brass rings.

'A hundred dollars,' the Mongolian said. He was not a man to be swayed from his purpose.

'Big mistake,' Alice's manager said as best he could.

'A hundred dollars,' the Mongolian said, 'O.K.'

'*You* are making a big mistake,' Alice's manager said.

The Mongolian hadn't realised that this was what he had meant. He had thought Alice's manager had been apologising. He brought the kukri down on to the glass table, passing in midflight through Alice's manager's hand, and chopped off all his fingers.

'Live round here,' the Mongolian said before the look on the manager's face changed to screaming. He tapped at his massive chest with his thumbnail, 'Be back.' He glanced at the mournful fingers on the glass display counter and went out.

Alice's manager's assistant rang first Hot Time Alice, who rang the men on the hill, who made a suggestion, and then he rang the hospital. He could not decide what the men on the hill, what Alice, and in that order, what the manager would expect him to do with the fingers so, being a cautious man who wanted to offend no one, he left them where the manager had left them, on the glass counter.

The Mongolian went next door, collected his hundred dollars without argument—the screaming coming from next door and the blood on the kukri helped the owner decide without undue fuss—and decided to take a break.

'Mr—?' Constable Cho asked politely. The man had been drinking and he kept belching fumes that made the Constable's eyes water.

'Skilbeck,' the man slurred. Constable Cho wrote down *Gilpeck*. 'Goddamned stupid—bitch has walked off.' He belched.

Constable Cho wrote, 'Missing person—'

'Goddamn bitch,' Mr Skilbeck said, 'Motherfucken airline lost the motherfucken luggage and this son-of-a-damn-poor-bitch hasn't got anywhere to stay until—'

'Have you got money?' Constable Cho asked. He thought—

'Motherfucken Traveller's Cheques,' the man said. 'Got mother—'

'Please don't use language,' Constable Cho said. 'Your wife's lost?'

'Right.'

Constable Cho glanced back at the desks. Spencer and Auden had gone out to investigate another report from the rickshaw driver that he had been bashed. It was the same rickshaw driver every night. Feiffer and Sun were out with the murders in Cuttlefish Lane, and Constable Lee had gone round to the street water taps to leave a police sign saying the water was off and wouldn't be turned on again until further notice. He didn't count Minnie Oh because he thought it wasn't a woman's business and he thought the language would shock her. He didn't have an overwhelming urge for Minnie Oh, but he didn't want her to think he condoned swearing.

He said to the man, 'Leave it an hour, Mr Gilpeck, and if your wife's in this district she'll come here.'

Mr Skilbeck belched, shrugged, and belched again, then went out.

Constable Cho wiped his eyes and thought he had handled that very well. He put the report in the Pending tray which, on principle, no one ever looked at.

'Goddamned illiterate Chink cop,' Mr Skilbeck said in the street and belched again. He lurched off to find a bar.

He finally found one named *Alice's* on the corner of Wanchai Street and Icehouse Street and went in.

Feiffer found a bar with a window looking out on Cat Street and waited for the food stalls to open for the night.

The manager's office had a framed advertisement for a film called *In Her Arms* with Warner Baxter and Elissa Landi and Paul Cavanagh (in smaller type) and an Alfred Hitchcock movie called *Suspicion*.

Each time they kissed ... the Warner Baxter movie warned, *there was the thrill of love ... THE THREAT OF MURDER!* It had Sir Cedric Hardwicke in it and Cary Grant and Joan Fontaine.

The other one said, *Oriental pride yields to Parisian kisses in a duel of male might and female charm ... an exotic drama of love's sublime cruelty.* O'Yee thought, 'My wife would like that one.'

'Have you got your gun?' the manager asked. He kept his voice low and craned forward eagerly like a rancher buying a fast-draw killer. In *Billy the Kid*, O'Yee thought, *Starring Johnny Mack Brown, Wallace Beery and Lucille Powers, a King Vidor Production, a Metro-Goldwyn-Mayer All Talking Picture.*

'I'm not a gunfighter,' O'Yee said, 'I represent law and order.' *High Noon starring Gary Cooper and Grace Kelly directed by Fred Zinnerman and a Stanley Kramer Production.*

'I don't want to get robbed,' the manager said. *Howard Hawks' Great Production Red River Greatest Spectacle Ever starring John Wayne and—*

'I've seen the film you've got on: *McQ*. All the cops get killed.'

'You'll be out in the cashier's box and I expect you to stop me getting robbed,' the manager said sourly. 'You've got no right to get killed.'

O'Yee nodded. It felt less and less like a movie by the moment. He took his coat off and satisfied the manager's eager stare that there was indeed a revolver under there, took his shoulder holster off and handed the gun to the manager. He was about to say, 'Does that make you feel better?' when the manager covered the gun with his silk pocket handkerchief and was gone, carrying the wrapped-up .38 out to the cashier's box like an offering to an altar.

'An exotic drama of—' O'Yee read and went out to hold the ranch.

* * *

Feiffer looked at his watch. It was nine o'clock. People came drifting in groups from Hanford Road and Wyang Street towards the opening food stalls. A few family members sat themselves down in front of their father's or husband's or brother's stalls to give the impression of a desirable rendezvous, but most of the drifters were on their evening meal break and knew their favourite stall or where they could get quick service or other woodcarvers or shoemakers or toy-assemblers might be found and they made for them. Or they did not own their own woodcarving, shoemaking or toy-assembly business, were employees and wanted to keep well away from other woodcarvers, shoemakers or toy-assemblers. The smell from the charcoal fires and the cooking meat and noodles and bamboo shoots rose with the grey smoke as the cooks set to work and the rice bowls and chopsticks were laid out on wooden counters. Feiffer ordered another beer from the bar owner and motioned him to bring it over.

The bar owner was a large, fat Northern Chinese named Lop with puffy eyes and a soiled napkin in the front pocket of his apron and he knew who Feiffer was.

'You know who I am,' Feiffer said.

The bar owner shook his head. He didn't know anything. He uncapped the bottle of Tiger beer and left it on the table.

'Just a minute,' Feiffer said.

The bar owner sniffed and turned back.

'You know who I am,' Feiffer said, 'I'm a police officer.'

The bar owner nodded resignedly. It took all kinds.

'I'm looking for someone.'

The bar owner nodded again. If he had been Jewish the nod would have meant, 'So what else is new?'

'Chen,' Feiffer said.

The bar owner, who spoke English, said, 'Smith.'

'Chen and Wang.'

'Smith and Jones.'

'They own a food stall.'

The bar owner shook his head.

'It isn't licensed.'

The bar owner recoiled in horror. He raised his eyebrows. He said, 'No?'

'I'm asking you to assist the police.'

The bar owner turned his gaze on to the street outside, then back to Feiffer. He shrugged. His shrug said he had looked, thought about it, and was totally dejected at the loss of his one chance in life to do his small part towards the maintenance of an ordered society and the triumph of good over evil. He lit a cigarette and put the dead match in Feiffer's ashtray.

'Don't want to get involved,' Feiffer said. 'You have to live around here.'

'Don't want to get involved,' the bar owner said. 'I have to live around here.'

'You're Northern Chinese.'

The bar owner nodded.

'First generation Hong Kong?'

The bar owner nodded again.

'Has Daddy got an entry permit?'

The bar owner nodded.

'Mummy?'

The bar owner nodded.

'So I can't pressure you?'

The bar owner shook his head.

'You're not going to tell me where Chen is?'

The bar owner shook his head.

'So you know him?'

The bar owner shook his head.

Feiffer switched to English. 'Do you want to tell me in English?'

The bar owner shook his head. He wasn't going to say 'No' or 'Yes' in another language. Some of the other customers were watching and they might not be as educated and bilingual as he and consequently get the wrong idea and come back tomorrow night and kill him.

'What's your name?' Feiffer said in Cantonese.
'Lop.'
Two of the customers left.
'No point in threatening you?'
The bar owner ran the soiled bar towel around Feiffer's table top and shook his head.
'Tax,' Feiffer said.
'What?' the bar owner said.
'I said, tax. I want to see your tax returns for the last three years and the accounting books, the petty cash sheet and the contents of the cash register, your bank books and an inventory of your possessions, the lease of this bar, your marriage certificate, your family's entry permits, your father's tax papers and the contents of your pockets. The pockets first.'
The bar owner looked at him.
'Turn out your pockets.'
The bar owner looked at the remaining customers.
'And then I want to see your stock and count the bottles and receipts, debts, liquor on account, cigarette records and I want to ask your customers if they've ever picked up girls in this bar and what your cut is and whether they were satisfied with the jig-jig.'
'Eastern end of Cat Street,' the bar owner said. 'Left hand side, behind the rice stall.'
'Forget about your tax,' Feiffer said.
'Chen's an illegal,' the bar owner said.
'Illegal immigrant?'
'Hmm.'
'Wang?'
'No.'
'Stall licence?'
'Forged.'
'By who?'
'No.'
'All right. Seen him tonight? Chen?'
'No.'

'Have you?'

'No!'

'Trouble?'

'Don't know.'

'Thank you very much.'

The bar owner nodded. He thought to say something.

'Don't say it.' Feiffer stood up.

The bar owner looked at the opened bottle of beer. 'Going to pay for it?'

'Didn't drink it.'

'Take it anyway.'

'I can't drink on duty,' Feiffer said. His tone said he found it a shocking and immoral suggestion.

'Not for drinking,' the bar owner said. 'Shove it up your arse!'

'He doesn't pay taxes,' Feiffer said loudly to the other customers. 'How can you associate with a man like this who's going to be investigated any moment?'

The other customers left.

'Warn Chen and I'll come back and slice your ears off,' Feiffer said to the bar owner and then he, too, left.

Hot Time Alice was at the hospital by the time they took her manager out from Casualty into the operating theatre for surgery. She asked the assistant what had happened and he told her. Alice said, 'Mongolian,' nodded, and filed the information away in a part of her jowl-heavy head where if the assistant had been filed he would have been searching for a lawyer to make a quick will.

'It wasn't my fault,' the assistant said. He was a thin, Hoklo speaking Southern Chinese from the boat people area of Hong Bay and he was beginning to wonder why he ever left the family vessel to waddle up on to dry land.

Alice moved her head very slowly from side to side. Her gold bangle earrings made a clinking noise like Mexican spurs on her stretched earlobes. She counted the rings on her fat fingers and then the diamonds in the rings and satisfied herself that so far all she had lost were a manager's four fingers. She said, 'Huhh,' which terrified the assistant by its basic lack of hard information, and began counting the carats in the diamonds on the rings she had already counted.

'What did he want? Money. How much? A lot.'

The assistant did not answer. He thought it might have been a complete conversation.

'Well?'

'A hundred,' the assistant said. 'We wouldn't give it to him. It isn't our money. It's yours. We wouldn't give your money away. Your money is—'

'He didn't chop your hand off?'

'He might have. He was going to. I was next. He would have—I wouldn't have given him the money if he had chopped off my whole—'

Alice made a grunting noise and took a cigarette from a pocket in her coat. It looked minute in her mouth, like an elephant using a toothpick, and when she inhaled the smoke did not come out again. It went inside that massive block of lard and was too scared to come back near the teeth in case they snapped at it.

'First,' Alice said, 'I decided we cut his balls off and let him bleed to death.' She shook her head, 'Second, I've got a Jap boy who says he can disembowel.'

The assistant tried to form a sympathetic smile.

'Third, I spoke to some friends,' Alice said. The assistant thought of the dark telephone lines terminating in a black room somewhere on Hanford Hill and his stomach contracted. 'Fourth, a decision has been made.'

The assistant forced a cheerful nod. He held his teeth tight together because they kept making a noise that sounded like he was cold. One of the hospital nuns came down the corridor and the assistant wanted to grasp her around her black cloth-covered knees and beg for refuge and a safe passage out to Cuba. 'Yes,' Alice said.

The nun halted in front of Alice. Alice stood up and towered over the minute creature.

I'm Sister Sung,' the nun who was a trained nurse said. 'Praise be to God your friend is all right.'

'Praise be to God,' Alice who was an atheist said. She looked at the assistant.

The assistant, who was a Buddhist, said, 'Praise be to God and our Lord Jesus Christ.'

'It was a terrible accident,' Sister Sung said. She motioned to the bench where Alice and the assistant had been sitting, 'Do sit down.'

'Thank you, Sister,' Alice said. She sat down.

The assistant remained standing. He was very respectful towards ladies.

'It was an accident?' the nun asked sweetly.

The assistant nodded.

'It was part of a crime against an honest business,' Alice said. 'I don't know how ordinary people can expect to go about their work in these times.'

'You'll call the police then?' the nun asked.

The assistant shook his head.

'As soon as I know my friend is out of danger,' Alice said, 'and I'd like to make a small donation to the St Paul de Chartres Hospital before I leave for their wonderful attention to him.'

'Your friend is out of danger,' Sister Sung said. 'We have no objection to a donation to help with our work.' She glanced at the assistant and then at Alice, 'You'll call the police now?'

'Yes, Sister,' Alice said. The assistant nodded enthusiastically.

Sister Sung considered Alice's veracity. 'You'll call them?' She prompted again, 'You know, Miss Ping—the cops?'

'We decided,' Alice said, 'we're going to call the police. I am, personally.' She nodded reassuringly at the diminutive religious person. 'Honest.'

Which, at exactly seven minutes past nine, Spencer, who answered the phone, found to his utter amazement to be true.

O'Yee and the manager were ensconced together inside the glass cashier's booth like two dressed Japanese dolls in a plastic container. O'Yee kept trying to concentrate on what the manager was saying—he was talking about ticket sales and the last thing O'Yee wanted if he didn't catch the Negro was a subsidiary charge of misappropriation—but the manager's attention kept straying to the Colt Airweight he still held in his silk handkerchief.

'There are front stalls and back stalls,' the manager said, 'don't mix them up and don't feel sorry for people who tell you they've got bad eyes and can't afford the better seats.'

O'Yee nodded. The manager kept running his hand along the outline of the gun under the handkerchief and patting the part where the cartridges were.

'What size is it?' the manager asked.

'What?'

'This.' He held up the gun.

'I'll have it back now if you don't mind,' O'Yee said. Being in the same glass box as a man in full cry with his fantasies made him feel uncomfortable.

'How many bullets?' the manager asked. He didn't give the gun back.

'Six,' O'Yee said. 'Can I please have my gun back?'

'Hmm,' the manager said. He had a quick, unutterably pleasurable vision of the thief of his life's work dying in convulsions outside his cinema like John Dillinger with a watering-can pattern of holes in him.

'Can I have my gun back, please?' O'Yee asked pleasantly. He did not want to upset someone who spent the greater part of his life wearing a bowtie in a dark cinema watching an unending procession of death and mayhem flickering on the screen.

'Don't get the tickets mixed up,' the manager said. He gave

the gun back reluctantly, still wrapped in the handkerchief. He gazed at it in warm anticipation.

O'Yee squeezed around until he was turned the other way and took the handkerchief off. He stuck the gun in the waistband of his trousers.

'I don't want the customers to see it,' the manager said totally untypically. It was a solo fantasy.

O'Yee put the gun on the shelf under the ticket counter and put an old fan magazine over it. He gave the handkerchief back to the manager.

'Will you be able to get at it?' the manager asked.

'I'm not a hired killer.'

'He's got a gun.'

'Then just let me get on with it, will you?'

The manager looked at him, summed him up. 'You won't want wages?'

'No.'

'I can let the cashier go? I was going to—I can let him go then?' He seemed very pleased he had hired the Capone gang to protect his establishment and simultaneously made an economy in staff. He thought his principals would be very satisfied.

'You can do what you like,' O'Yee said. 'That's your affair.'

The manager nodded. He adjusted his bowtie. He squeezed out of the glass cubicle. 'The cash box is just there. It's got change in it.'

'Thanks,' O'Yee said.

'One hundred dollars in ones, sixty dollars in tens and sixty-one dollars fifty in coins. Look at the change before you hand it to a customer.' He shut the glass door and surveyed his puppet. He mouthed, 'Ha!' enthusiastically against the soundproof glass. He glanced at the barrel of the gun protruding from under a picture of Gregory Peck on the front page of the fan magazine and thought that was who he had hired.

'It's all done with trick photography in the movies,' O'Yee said helplessly through the glass.

The manager's mouth said, 'What?' He opened the glass door with a sigh. 'What?'

'Nothing,' O'Yee said. The manager closed the door again.

'Fast draw,' O'Yee said to himself. He felt like a dinosaur in a glass display case. He remembered it wasn't the police who had shot John Dillinger outside a cinema in America. It had been the FBI. His parents, who still lived in San Francisco, had been clear about that: it was the FBI.

He thought, 'This is a hell of a life for a Chinese Irishman,' and opened up for business.

Mrs Skilbeck came back into the Police Station. She had half-filled her raffia bag with purchases. Auden said, 'Yes?' and asked if she wanted Minnie again. She said no, she didn't want Minnie again. She told him she had lost her husband. Her name was Mrs Skilbeck and did they have a report on him? 'Gilpeck?' Auden asked. He saw that name on the top form in the Pending tray. 'No,' Mrs Skilbeck said, 'Skilbeck.' 'He'll turn up,' Auden said hopefully, 'after all he's a big boy, isn't he?' and Mrs Skilbeck grunted.

He took her particulars and told her to come back in an hour to see if anything had happened.

Mrs Skilbeck said, *'Cops!'* and Auden wondered after she left what he had said wrong.

Chen and Wang's food stall, when Feiffer finally located it behind the rice stall, was closed. He went back to the rice stall and motioned to the owner.

'Only wholesale,' the owner said wearily in English. He had no intention of selling bowls of rice to European tourists and ending up in someone's photograph album or flickering away in colour through a Japanese projector on their parlour wall.

'I'm not buying,' Feiffer said in Chinese.

'Only wholesale,' the owner said.

Feiffer showed him his warrant card.

'Hmm,' the owner said, 'I haven't done anything.'

'I'm not interested in you.'
The owner nodded, unconvinced.
'The food stall behind you—'
'Don't know.'
'Anything?'
'Don't know.'
'Chen and Wang,' Feiffer said.
'Don't know,' the owner said.
'When does it open?'
'Don't know.'
'You're not in any trouble.'
'Good.' He contemplated Feiffer.

Feiffer contemplated the owner. He was a thin man surrounded by fat bags of rice. He had rice in his hair, in the front pocket of his apron, under his fingernails, on his face, and no doubt in his shoes. He looked very ricey.

'There's been a murder,' Feiffer said.

Rice came in pounds, kilos and hundredweights, maybe murders came in ones and twos. 'Not my business,' the owner said.

'What time do they usually open?'

'You open when there are customers,' the rice owner said. That was not giving anything away except the basic tenet of good business practice. 'No customers, no open.'

'If the stall isn't open the customers don't wait,' Feiffer said.

'If there is no demand a businessman loses profit by opening,' the rice owner countered.

'A good businessman anticipates demand,' Feiffer observed.

'Demand is a changeable thing.'

'A good businessman has no armour against unpredictability and change?' Feiffer asked. 'He is at the mercy of demand?'

'A good businessman anticipates demand,' the rice owner said.

'That's what I said.'

'True,' the rice owner said. He said, 'A good businessman does anticipate demand.'

'Well?'

The rice owner looked at him.

'When do they open?'

'Don't know,' the rice owner said.

'There have been two murders and we think someone at the stall may be able to assist with our enquiries.'

'Hmm,' the rice owner said.

Feiffer tried his man-in-the-society-of-his-fellows shot. 'A good businessman does his civic duty.'

'Hmm,' the rice owner said. He was not thinking about it.

'I don't want to make trouble for you,' Feiffer said.

'Of course not.'

'A good businessman keeps good records.'

The rice owner glanced past Feiffer. There were no customers at the moment. He leaned forward on his tabletop to continue the discussion. The man was quite bright for a European, he thought. 'A good businessman is obliged by the State to keep good records.'

'A good businessman would keep good records even if the State decayed away,' Feiffer said. He thought it was worthy of Confucius. 'A good businessman takes a pride in his work.'

'Yes,' the rice owner said. That was a good point.

'He would know who he has supplied the products of his business to without looking up the records the State obliges him to keep just because he is a good businessman.'

'True,' the rice owner said.

'You are the only rice supplier in this immediate area. So it is you who would have supplied rice to the food stall that is now closed because the owners are bad businessmen and do not anticipate demand.' He thought, this is driving me crazy.

'No,' the rice owner said.

'Your competitors supply it because you are a lousy businessman?' Feiffer asked.

'I supply it!'

'So you are a good businessman.'

'I am!'

'Ah,' Feiffer said. It was time for the crunch. He had trodden the paths of logic and inner purity carefully and now it was time for the reward. 'At what time do you supply the night's rice to the food stall of Chen and Wang?'

A slow smile creased the rice owner's face. It displaced several grains of rice from the corners of his mouth and turned him from a mere rice owner to a sage among the illiterate and unread masses.

'A good businessman keeps his transactions confidential.'

Feiffer closed his eyes. He felt his philosophical mantle drop from his shoulders. 'When do they buy their fucking rice?'

'Oh,' the rice owner said. He had been enjoying the meeting of like minds.

'Well?'

The rice owner looked at his ex-adversary and saw only a mere European.

'Don't know,' the rice owner said.

Feiffer drew a deep breath. He looked away from the rice owner's face to avoid doing it violence and saw that the food stall of Chen and Wang had been open for some time. Customers sat on stools around it munching their suppers in epicurean peace and clicking their chopsticks.

'A good businessman—' the rice owner began in a kindly tone.

'Go to hell!' Feiffer said.

The rice owner looked disappointed and rejected. He fixed Feiffer with a sad smile, thought that such was life, and went back to his rice bags.

'I've lost my wife,' Mr Skilbeck said.

'Oh,' Apricot Tang Lee said, 'poor boy.'

'Lost her.'

Apricot Tang Lee poured him another drink from the bottle on the table.

'Yeah,' Mr Skilbeck said. 'She's gone.'
'She dead?' Apricot Tang Lee asked. She poured Mr Skilbeck another drink.
'Gone,' Mr Skilbeck said. 'I don't care.' He looked at Apricot Tang Lee's breasts, 'What's your name?'
'Apricot.'
'That's nice,' Mr Skilbeck said. He leaned back in his chair and downed the drink. *Alice's* was almost three quarters full, what he could see of it in the gloom of the dimmed lights. The tables were up on little platforms around the walls with bamboo curtains dividing them off from the ones in the centre of the floor. 'You're nice,' he said again. 'I've always liked Chinese girls.'
Apricot laid her hand on Mr Skilbeck's crotch. 'Chinese girls know how to treat a man,' Mr Skilbeck said.
'Hong Kong girl like American man,' Apricot said. She ran her other hand across Mr Skilbeck's shoulders and then over his bald head, 'Hong Kong girl Apricot like smooth head.' She stroked his cheek, 'Whiskers.' She giggled.
'Stupid bitch,' Mr Skilbeck said. He looked at Apricot Tang Lee's breasts under her imitation silk cheong sam top that ended in a mini skirt, 'My wife—stupid bitch.'
'I got long leg,' Apricot Tang Lee said. She pulled the hem of her skirt back under the table and twisted her toes from left to right, 'See?'
Mr Skilbeck drew a deep breath, then let it out in a whisky-rubbery sound.
'Funny!' Apricot Tang Lee said and giggled.
Mr Skilbeck did it again.
'This's a nice place you've got here,' Mr Skilbeck said heavily. What he could see of it looked dim and gloomy and sequined. Nice. 'This all there is of it?'
'Rooms upstairs,' Apricot said. She poured him another drink. 'Rooms for very naughty boys.'
Mr Skilbeck looked at her breasts again.
'Nice,' Apricot Tang Lee said.

'Yeah.' He downed the drink and looked at Apricot Tang Lee's legs and breasts. He thought this was a nice place. He thought, American women—'American women,' Mr Skilbeck said definitively, 'are stupid bitches.' He sniffed. 'It has been my experience, having been married to one for three thousand years, that American women are stupid bitches.' There was another drink in front of him and he drank it.

'You American from—'

'New Jersey,' Mr Skilbeck said, 'I'm from New Jersey. Have you ever been to New Jersey?'

Apricot Tang Lee shook her head.

'The men from New Jersey,' Mr Skilbeck said, 'are very good lovers, but they have the problem of marrying stupid bitches from New Jersey. All the women from New Jersey are stupid bitches who get married to you and are stupid bitches who get married—' He forgot what he was trying to say. 'I forgot what I was trying to say.'

'New Jersey man good lover?'

'Right.'

'O.K.' Apricot said.

'Right,' Mr Skilbeck said.

Apricot nodded and flexed her pectoral muscles.

'Right,' Mr Skilbeck said, 'this is a very interesting conversation.' He poured himself a drink, 'Don't you drink?'

'Very bad for lady,' Apricot Tang Lee said. 'Too strong. For strong New Jersey man.'

'Sensible,' Mr Skilbeck said. He nodded and nodded again, kept on nodding, managed to stop nodding and said, 'Right.'

Apricot Tang Lee raised her eyes heavenward at the barman. The barman raised his eyes heavenward at Apricot Tang Lee.

'Do you take Traveller's Cheques?' Mr Skilbeck asked. He said quickly, reassuringly, 'American money.'

Apricot Tang Lee opened her mouth to say yes.

'American women drink too much,' Mr Skilbeck said, 'they're always drinking too much. Drink, drink, drink, drink, drink, yell, yell, yell, yell, shout, shout, shout, shout, bitch,

bitch, bitch, nag, nag, nag, nag, bitch, bitch, bitch, bitch, and they get lost. Stupid bitches. I like Chinese girls.'

Apricot Tang Lee sighed to herself and smiled sympathetically at Mr Skilbeck.

'What's your name, honey?' Mr Skilbeck asked.

'Apricot.'

Half a dozen sailors from the American destroyer in the harbour came in making a lot of noise to show they were at home in bars and dancehalls. They took a table in the centre of the floor.

'None of your watered down shit,' the leader, a tall Negro, shouted to the barman. 'Good stuff. Scotch. From Scotland, England.'

Apricot Tang Lee glanced at the sailors.

'I was in the Navy,' Mr Skilbeck said. 'In the Korean war. Things I could tell you.' He said, 'I was in the Navy,' and yelled across the floor to the Negro, 'What do you say, Captain?'

The Negro looked over. He said, 'Hi,' and went back to his conversation with the others. A couple of hostesses came over and sat with them.

'What do you say, brother?' Mr Skilbeck, who watched a lot of television at home, yelled over, 'Right on!'

The Negro raised his hand in a Vee sign.

'Brother!' Mr Skilbeck said.

'Yeah,' the Negro said and turned away to the girls. Mr Skilbeck heard him say, 'I got a lotta money coming whenever I want to pick it up,' and Mr Skilbeck said to Apricot Tang Lee, 'I gotta lotta money too.'

'I'm a kinda movie star,' the Negro said and guffawed with laughter.

'I gotta lotta—' Mr Skilbeck began. Apricot watched the sailors. 'I've got money,' Mr Skilbeck said.

'Fifty bucks,' Apricot said. Someone came through the door and glanced at her as he went past towards the back rooms. She said, 'Good evening, Inspector Spencer.'

'Cop!' someone in the Negro's party said and they fell silent and looked at their drinks, their girls, their hands, their tabletop, the walls.

'Hullo,' Spencer said. Feiffer had taken him on a tour of the bars and dancehalls on his first day, but he couldn't remember all the names, 'Is Miss Ping in?'

'Miss Alice is in her office,' Apricot said in Cantonese.

'No one in the rooms upstairs I trust?' Spencer said.

Apricot shook her little head so hard her long hair flew out and whisked painfully across Mr Skilbeck's fragile eyes.

'Not while I'm here anyway,' Spencer said. He glanced at the party of sailors.

'I'm going out to get some money,' the Negro said. He got up and left.

Spencer looked at Mr Skilbeck. Mr Skilbeck smiled absently at him.

'Office?' Spencer confirmed.

Apricot nodded.

Mr Skilbeck nodded.

Spencer went past the sailors towards the office.

'Have a drink,' Apricot Tang Lee said. She poured a quick shot for Mr Skilbeck. She was so annoyed she spilled most of it on the table.

'I've got bad eyes,' the little old Chinese lady said to O'Yee, 'I can't read the subtitles in the front.'

'Go to the back then,' O'Yee said. He handed her a front stalls ticket for the money she had counted out on the countertop.

'Thank you, thank you,' the little old Chinese lady said eagerly. She scuttled towards the manager and the curtained doorway, handed him the ticket, and told him what the nice young man in the cashier's booth had said.

The manager moved back the curtain and the little old Chinese lady went in happily. The manager looked daggers at the nice young man in the cashier's booth.

'I've got bad eyes too,' the little old Chinese man next in the queue behind the little old Chinese lady said. He counted out the exact price of a front stalls ticket.

'Not twice in a row,' O'Yee said. 'You must think I'm stupid.'

Tears appeared in the little old Chinese man's eyes. 'We're married,' he said plaintively, 'We couldn't—'

'O.K.,' O'Yee said. He thought this was a hard job for a man who suffered from an excess of kind-heartedness. He looked up at the next customer in the queue. The next customer was a teenage boy who wore no glasses, looked in the pink of health and prime condition and handed him a ten dollar note.

'Front or back?' O'Yee asked confidently.

The healthy specimen of a teenage boy thought for a moment.

'What did you sell my grandfather and grandmother?' he asked, 'I'll sit with them.'

The Negro went out of *Alice's*, crossed over Icehouse Street, and turned into Hong Bay Beach Lane near the Bus Station. He went into the first novelty shop in the lane and purchased three plastic bow and arrow sets, a plastic speedcar made in Taiwan, a Ludo and Chess set made out of cardboard with little paper markers, a magnetic Scrabble game set in a green plastic travel wallet, a black plastic imitation of a Colt Government Model .45 calibre automatic pistol, three Chinese dolls with fixed expressions of schizophrenic withdrawal and no clothes on, and a rubber snake with green eyes and yellow fangs. The girl assistant put it all in a paper bag for him.

Back in Icehouse Street he deposited everything except the pistol into the first litter bin he saw and walked up the road to see what was on at the movies.

Auden leaned back in his wooden chair in the Yellowthread Street Police Station and contemplated the finished accident report still in his typewriter. All he had to do was sign it. He contemplated the final flourish of a signature and thought it wasn't a bad typing job. He glanced at the open door to the street. A few people went by, one way and the other, going or coming to or from places, but none of them seemed in dire need of the police. No one came in with a problem. Delicious, that was the word that crossed Auden's mind. It was a delicious feeling that all was right with the world. The accident report from last night had been typed up. It would go to the insurance company. There would be no court case; life, limb or serious property damage had not been involved, and Minnie Oh was down the corridor in her office. She might even feel all was so well with her world to come out and talk to him while the new opposition, Spencer, was away in the brothel centre of the Orient.

Auden felt a delicious feeling of well-being. It was ten o'clock and he had only been called out once (for the lunatic rickshaw man who should have been bashed for falsely claiming he had been bashed) since he had come on duty, and Minnie Oh might wander out on her black high heels on her long, long legs and all was well.

He decided in his perfect lassitude to clean his gun. He took it out from his top drawer in its Berns-Martin upside-down holster he had ordered all the way from America and looked at it lovingly.

Non-regulation, it was a Colt Python with a two-and-a-half-inch barrel, and, regulation, the first chamber had been loaded with a .38. If Auden ever had to shoot anyone the .38 was what the Department decreed it should be done with, but in the next chamber—Auden had decided in an imaginative moment that the second shot would not be to save the Department's reputation but to save Auden's life—the cartridge was a .357 magnum.

In the new movie at the Peacock Auden had seen the other night, John Wayne had blasted a hired assassin with a magnum and Auden had secretly quivered with excitement in his seat.

He clicked out the cylinder and checked that the .38 round

was next up to the hammer and the .357 was immediately after it.

He pointed the weapon at the wall and said, 'Wallop!' God, he felt deliciously idle ...

He yawned.

'Chen?' Feiffer asked Chen quietly. The photograph had been a good one.

Chen went on cooking pork in his circular wok over a charcoal fire. One of the eaters sitting next to Feiffer put his half-finished meal down on the counter and decided to leave.

'Where's your partner Mr Wang?' Feiffer asked. He glanced at the licence card tacked up to one of the upright supports of the wooden stall. It said Chen and Wang and the photos were the same. The man cooking was Mr Chen, the husband, and without too much doubt, the axeman.

'Do you want a meal?' Chen asked without turning around.

Feiffer thought, 'My Cantonese accent isn't that good. He knows who I am.'

Chen went on cooking the pork, flicking minute quantities of peanut oil into the wok to keep the pork pieces sizzling.

'No,' Feiffer said, 'I want you. I'm a Police Inspector.'

There were three other customers sitting and standing at the stall and they too decided to leave. They went over to the rice owner's stall and struck up an earnest conversation.

'Your customers have gone,' Feiffer said. He thought he could vault over the bench table if Chen made a run for it. He said, 'I think you and I have something to discuss, don't we?'

Chen nodded. He kept his eyes on the frying pork and flicked a little more peanut oil into the wok. He turned and gazed at Feiffer and nodded again. Feiffer thought he was deciding something.

'No customers,' Chen said. His voice sounded very sad and disappointed. He emptied the half-fried pork into a bowl by the side of the fire and ladled oil into the wok. He held the wok carefully and swirled the oil about in it until it began to boil. Feiffer put his hand under his coat for his pistol.

'Don't do anything silly,' Feiffer said, 'there's no reason why we can't settle this without trouble.'

Chen nodded. He looked down at the boiling oil and then at the long carving knife he used for the pork.

'You're not going to be silly,' Feiffer said. His hand closed around the butt of the Colt Airweight and moved it slightly in its leather holster.

'I'm an illegal,' Chen said. He nodded towards the licence card, 'That's forged. I haven't got a licence.'

'Yes.'

He was not a young man and Feiffer saw that his back was beginning to stoop, and the way he held the wok suggested that, increasingly, he found things getting heavier. He put the wok down on the charcoal fire and the oil bubbled furiously. He rubbed at his chin with a bony hand. Then he picked the wok up again and went on with his work.

'You're not cooking anything in that,' Feiffer said, 'I think you had better pour the oil out and we'll have a chat.'

'I came over from Canton,' Chen said, 'I swam the Pearl River. I didn't register because the government wasn't accepting any more refugees.' He jerked his head at the licence card again, 'Wang said we could make money because if we weren't registered we wouldn't pay taxes. That's why it's such a bad location.'

'Behind the rice stall.'

'Hmm.' He nodded.

'Was Wang registered?'

He thought Chen made a bitter smile. 'He was Hong Kong born. He said he was my friend. We were partners. He took seventy per cent because he was hiding me and he got the forged licence. He was sleeping with my wife.' He said quickly, 'She wasn't an illegal—just me. Wang introduced me to her and said she would be a good wife.'

'Was he sleeping with her tonight?' Feiffer asked. He kept

his eyes on the boiling oil, the knife, and on the tension in Chen's hands and elbows.

'Oh, yes,' Chen said. The oil was simmering hot. Feiffer wondered how he could hold the wok. He thought the man probably didn't even feel it. 'Oh, yes,' Chen said, 'Oh, yes.'

'And you killed them both?'

'Oh, yes,' Chen said. 'Yes, I did that.'

'You know you'll have to come with me?'

'Oh, yes.'

'Come on then.'

'All right,' Chen said and threw the boiling oil at him.

In that instant, Feiffer ducked and the oil passed to one side of him, Chen dropped the wok and reached for his knife, Feiffer yanked at the pistol and jammed it in the leather of the holster and his shirt and Chen leapt over the back wall of the wooden stall and began running towards him.

Feiffer yanked at the gun in the crouching position and overbalanced. He fell against a stool and brought it down as Chen went past him with the knife poised in the air. He went towards the rice stall and the talkers. The talkers scattered. Feiffer yelled, 'Stop him!' and the talkers, without hesitation, got out of Chen's way. He collided with the rice owner's stall and brought an opened bag of rice crashing down from a weighing machine to one side of the counter and slipped in the cascade of grains.

Feiffer got to his feet and ran after him. Somehow, Chen seemed caught up in the avalanche of rice. He kicked at it and took wild swipes in the air with his knife. Feiffer's left hand began to hurt. There was oil on it, sizzling the hairs above his fingers and on his wrist. He tried to wipe it away with his other hand. Chen kicked at the near empty rice sack and yelled, 'I'll kill you!' and just then the rice owner knocked him cold with a metal saucepan.

'He killed two people,' Feiffer told the rice owner when he finally managed to rearrange his holster, verify that the oil had not burned through a vital artery, and make it over to where

Chen lay stretched out like a poisoned rat in a grain warehouse.

'He ruined my rice,' the rice owner said, 'I'll expect compensation.'

Feiffer felt a great glow of fraternal love and gratitude towards the rice owner flow over him. 'You'll probably get a medal.'

'Just the compensation,' the rice owner said. 'A good businessman protects the reputation of his neighbourhood.'

Feiffer said—Feiffer put his mind in order and said—Feiffer pontificated, 'A good businessman—' but the rice owner put up his hand like a traffic policeman to stop him.

'No,' the rice owner said. He considered Feiffer carefully and judiciously. He was sorry he had ever lowered himself to intellectual dispute with him, 'No.'

The rice owner said, 'I just don't think you're that bright,' and commenced saving what he could of his ruined stock.

The rush for water from the single rationed tap in the western section of Hong Bay would start in the morning, as it would for the single taps in the northern, southern and eastern areas.

By each of the taps a Landrover carrying members of the Police Riot Squad from their headquarters near the border at Fanling got into position well in advance.

They noted that the constables from Yellowthread Street had signposted the taps, warning about the shortage, and they expected a quiet night.

It suited them, they were due to come off duty before dawn, and the day shift from Fanling would have the hard part. They sat around picking broken threads from their rattan shields and talking about Saturday's racemeeting at Happy Valley.

Mr Skilbeck was very, very drunk and he was doing his best to rape Apricot Tang Lee. That is to say, he said in a very loud voice that if she wasn't going to take him upstairs he was damn well going to rape her and Chinese women were no different from New Jersey women and you might as well take it by force because you never got anywhere being nice.

The sailors, one of whom was also from New Jersey and who paid alimony to an address there he had spent twenty years in the Navy paying for, all nodded and said, 'Yeah, get on with it!' and shot threatening glances at the barman.

The barman polished glasses and looked the other way.

'Do me a favour,' Hot Time Alice said to Spencer at the door of her office. No one knew better than she that drinking provoked the desire but took away from the performance, 'Go and arrest that drunk.'

Spencer looked over at Skilbeck. Apricot had taken refuge under the table and Skilbeck was looking under the tablecloth—which had the tabletop between it and Apricot—for the object of his rapine.

'I don't want you to do anything private about this Mongolian thing, Alice,' Spencer said, 'it's a police matter.'

'I reported it, didn't I?' She still seemed a little surprised about it herself.

'Yes,' Spencer said, 'Leave it to us. We'll handle it.'

'Hmm,' Alice said. She seemed far from happy. The thought of the Jap boy who said he could disembowel had grown on her since the decision from Hanford Hill. She said, 'It's a pity.'

'Alice—' Spencer said. On the way out he arrested Mr Skilbeck.

O'Yee saw the Negro sailor in the queue. There were two schoolgirls—one European and one Chinese—a young man with glasses, his girlfriend, someone's mother and then the Negro. O'Yee glanced down at Gregory Peck and the barrel of the Colt that came out at about the right ear. The Negro was tall and thin and towered over the young man, his girlfriend and someone's mother.

The Chinese schoolgirl said, 'Front or back?' to her European friend and her friend said, 'Can we afford back stalls?'

They both consulted their purses.

O'Yee waited for them to decide and watched the Negro. The Negro read a poster on the wall nonchalantly. O'Yee looked for gun bulges under his tunic, but someone's mother moved impatiently and blocked him out.

The Chinese schoolgirl said, 'Back stalls,' and O'Yee gave her the ticket and the wrong change.

'Pardon me,' the Chinese schoolgirl said.

O'Yee gave her the right change.

'Back stalls,' the European girl said. Her friend read the starting times of the features near the poster and said, 'Come on, Mary.'

O'Yee gave Mary her ticket and the right change.

The young man with glasses disengaged his girlfriend from the line and said, 'Two back stalls,' and handed O'Yee eight one-dollar notes and change.

O'Yee clicked out two tickets from the machine on the benchtop.

The young man said, 'I gave you the right money.'

'Did I shortchange you?'

'No. But you didn't count it.'

'I trust you,' O'Yee said. He glanced around someone's mother at the Negro. The Negro caught his eye, held it curiously and then looked away.

'O.K.' the young man said. He thought that was no way to make a profit. He went over to his girlfriend, said something about the changing state of the world and hope for tomorrow based on mutual trust and respect, and took her inside.

The gun was under Gregory Peck's face. O'Yee had a sudden doubt that he could get his hand around the butt fast enough and what if the hammer caught in the pages of the magazine or—

'Please,' someone's mother said abruptly, 'Money, ticket.'

O'Yee gave her a ticket.

'Front stalls,' someone's mother said, 'I'm not paying more

just because you give me the wrong ticket. I asked for front stalls—'

'It's all right,' O'Yee said. The Negro began feeling in his pocket for something. O'Yee thought that the gun would point at his face because that was almost the only part visible above the cashier's box.

'No,' someone's mother said, 'it's a trick to get more money out of people who can't afford it. I haven't see you here before. You're not the right cashier.'

O'Yee watched the Negro. He said, 'I'm new.'

'Are you sure you work here?'

The Negro looked curious. He couldn't understand a word of Cantonese but he knew from the tone that something was wrong.

'We're having a sale on back stall tickets,' O'Yee said. 'Take it with our compliments.'

'Well—' someone's mother said. She glanced behind her at the Negro. The Negro raised his eyebrows and wondered if they were talking about him. Someone's mother said something to him in Cantonese and he smiled reassuringly at her and moved to the head of the queue as someone's mother went muttering to herself towards the entrance.

O'Yee put his hand on his gun and got the butt, slid it out from under Gregory Peck's ear and held it pointing at the floor by his side.

'Do you speak English?' the Negro asked very slowly and carefully.

'Yes.'

'I want to ask you something.' He glanced behind him: he was the only customer. There was time.

'Go ahead.'

'Has the movie got, ah—' The Negro thought for the word, 'Is it in English? You know, um—'

'Subtitles,' O'Yee offered. He curled his finger around the trigger of his revolver and felt the spring pressure on it.

'Yeah.'

'It's in English. The subtitles are in Chinese.'

'But John Wayne talks in English?'

'Yes.'

'Great,' the Negro said, 'Good movie. John Wayne always makes good movies. Is this the one where all the cops get killed and John Wayne shoots it out on a beach and kills the detective?'

'That's the one,' O'Yee said. He cocked the hammer. It made a faint clicking sound. The cartridge under the claw of the hammer waited to be consummated.

'Great movie,' the Negro said. He handed over a ten dollar note, 'Is that O.K. for the ticket?'

O'Yee looked at the banknote lying on the counter. He took it up with his left hand, put it in the cashbox with his left hand, extracted the change with his left hand, and punched out the ticket with his left hand.

'What's wrong with your other hand?' the Negro asked politely, 'Hurt it?'

'Yeah,' O'Yee said.

'Bad luck,' the Negro said. He took his ticket, glanced at the poster of John Wayne slaughtering multitudes with the gleeful anticipation of a man who knew there were over two hundred John Wayne movies to catch up with all over the world, and went inside.

He wasn't the one.

There was a little swing-out stool top in the cashier's booth against the wall behind him. O'Yee swung it out and sat down.

When he came upstairs from the detention cells Feiffer's phone was ringing. He picked it up and said, 'Feiffer.'

'Hullo, Feiffer.' It was his wife. There was the sound of television in the background. A quiz show. Quiz shows bored his wife to distraction. He was the distraction.

'Hi.'

'How's it going?'

'Fine, fine.'

'Have you been out tonight?'

'I have, as a matter of fact. I met all sorts of interesting people.'

'One of your long philosophical discussions?'

'Two or three.'

'And?'

'How are you anyway?' Feiffer asked. 'There's a quiz show on television. Am I right?'

'A lightweight animal starting with O.'

'An ounce,' Feiffer said. 'It's a sort of lynx.'

'You make me sick.'

'It's like a snow leopard only smaller.'

'You looked it up.'

'How could I have done that? I've been out arresting a double murderer.'

'Are you hurt?'

'No.'

'Are you sure?'

'I'm sure.' He glanced at his coatsleeve, 'I got a stain on my coat but it should come off.'

Her tone changed. It sounded as though she switched the television off, 'Not blood, Harry?'

'Peanut oil.'

'I wish to God you'd buy a new suit. That one looks like Orson Welles last wore it in *Ferry to Hong Kong*.'

'I like it. It makes me look weatherbeaten and cynical.'

'You are weatherbeaten and cynical. You won't be working overtime with your murderer?'

'You'll be delighted to know he made a full confession. He's sitting comfortably downstairs in the cells waiting for the Magistrate. I'll be home on time.'

'I'm glad.'

'What time does your quiz show finish?'

'Any moment. I just thought I'd ring you up and tell you about the lightweight animal. I wish I hadn't.'

'Do you love me?' Feiffer asked. Auden looked over from

his desk and shook his head. He said, 'Tell her that I love her.'

'Auden says he loves you.'

'Tell him to get knotted.'

'She says to get knotted.'

'Harry?'

'Yes?'

'I do love you.'

'What's on after the quiz show?'

'*The Maltese Falcon.* The one about Philip Marlowe or Sam Spade—Humphrey Bogart.'

'Take notes.'

'Goodnight, Harry.'

'Goodnight. I'll see you in the morning.'

'Harry?'

'Yes?'

'You do love me, don't you?'

'Yes.'

'Goodnight.'

'Goodnight.' He put the receiver back gently on its cradle and thought about his wife.

'That was Nicola,' Auden said. He smiled enviously.

Feiffer looked at him. He nodded his head in admiration. 'You ought to be a detective,' he said to Auden.

'Get knotted,' Auden said.

Constable Cho was out when Spencer brought Mr Skilbeck in, so although he did not see anyone he knew at the Police Station he knew the Police Station.

He said, 'I'm not staying here!' and hit Spencer in the stomach. Spencer fell back against the door jamb and almost toppled down the front steps of the Station. He had a look of utter surprise on his face. He stared up at Mr Skilbeck with the look of surprise still on his face and said, 'You were docile—'

'I'm not staying here!' Mr Skilbeck, who was not in the right humour to discuss treachery with British cops, said.

He said, 'Apricot—it was all your fault!'

'Hey—' Spencer said. He began to get up. He felt very surprised that someone had hit him in the stomach. After actually having a crime reported to him by Hot Time Alice Ping he had thought it was going to be such a good night. 'Hey—' Spencer said.

'Oh, no,' Mr Skilbeck said and drew back his fist to hit him again.

'Wait—' Spencer suggested reasonably. He was sure that if he could actually talk to Alice Ping he could easily reason with a—

'They lost my goddamned luggage in goddamned Djarkarta,' Mr Skilbeck said.

Detective Inspector Auden thought that was a very odd thing to say after you had just assaulted a police officer, but he did not think about it too long. He hit Mr Skilbeck and handcuffed him on the floor.

'What'd he say?' he asked Spencer.

'I don't know,' Spencer said. 'He was very docile up till now.' Mr Skilbeck had cried in the back of Spencer's car and Spencer had had to get the driver to stop to agree with him that no normal human being in his sane mind would ever really want to leave the comforts and tranquillity of New Jersey anyway.

'Where's New Jersey?' Spencer asked Auden.

'In America.'

Spencer looked down at Mr Skilbeck. Tears were in Mr Skilbeck's eyes and he was making short frustrated grunts and banging his forehead on the floor.

'I can't understand it at all,' Detective Inspector Spencer said. 'It must be a thoroughly peculiar place.'

He glanced down at Mr Skilbeck, absolutely at a loss to understand him.

O'Yee looked at his watch. The John Wayne movie was half through. The young man and his girlfriend came out with an expression of set, different purpose on their collective faces and went quickly—almost indecently orgiastically, O'Yee thought—into the first taxi that passed. The young man gave frantic instructions to the driver and fell back upon his girl-friend as the taxi sped away. A flurry of blank gunshots cracked out from inside the cinema as John Wayne, impervious to lead, shot it out with the crooked detective and the crooked detective shot it out with John Wayne.

No one was coming. O'Yee lit a cigarette and fished around under the bench for an ashtray. He found one, and moved his gun to one corner out of the way of it. He looked up into the muzzle of the biggest pistol he had ever seen in his life.

The Negro said, 'I didn't like the movie.'

O'Yee looked at him.

The Negro said, 'I'm going to blow your face off.'

Constable Lee unlocked Mr Skilbeck's handcuffs, shoved him into the second detention cell, closed the metal door swiftly, and turned the key.

The Negro said, 'I want money.'

The Negro said, 'Did you hear what I said?'

O'Yee nodded.

'Do it with your good hand,' the Negro said. He smiled evilly and pushed the muzzle of the gun a few inches closer to O'Yee's left eye.

'Listen—'

'Nothing. Money. Or Bang!'

'I'm a—' O'Yee tried. His voice sounded tinny. He cleared his throat, 'I'm a—'

'We've all got problems,' the Negro said. 'Yours is me. Money!'

O'Yee couldn't remember where his gun was on the bench. He couldn't remember if it was under Gregory Peck's ear or on top of it or under the ashtray or beside it. The black eye of the pistol barrel watched his eye. O'Yee's eye was afraid to look down.

'I'm a—' O'Yee said. He cleared his throat, 'Listen—' O'Yee said.

'O.K.' the Negro said. 'You're dead.'

'I'm a police officer!' O'Yee got out. It sounded less like the way John Wayne said it to state a fact of terrifying proportions than a plea that O'Yee had seven children and an ancient mother to support.

'What?' the Negro said.

'I'm a police officer,' O'Yee said more calmly. He didn't want to upset anyone. 'I haven't got a bad hand.'

'You've got a gun,' the Negro said. His eyes flickered down to the wall of the cashier's booth at about his groin level. Something metal that could go through walls and groins as if they were not there was pointing at him behind it.

'Yeah,' O'Yee said. He swallowed and hoped. 'Yeah!' he said again, 'Reach for the sky!'

A metamorphosis took place before O'Yee's eyes. The black eye of the pistol blinked, shook its head, blinked again, and then did a nose dive to the ground. It made a snapping sound as it hit the concrete floor. The Negro stepped back, blinked his own eyes, and shouted, 'Don't shoot!'

'O.K.,' O'Yee said benevolently. He nodded—just like John Wayne—unlocked the door of the cashier's booth carefully and calmly—just like John Wayne—and stepped out purposefully and firmly to make his arrest.

'Don't kill me!' the Negro said. He threw himself against the poster on the wall with his legs spreadeagled to be searched.

'O.K.,' O'Yee said, and searched him.

'Don't kill me,' the Negro said quietly as O'Yee handcuffed him. The manager came out and saw the scene.

'Call the Station,' O'Yee said.

The Negro said to the manager, 'Tell him not to kill me.'

The manager hesitated.

'Call the Station,' O'Yee said. 'I got him.'

The manager scuttled away.

'It wasn't a real gun,' the Negro said pleadingly. 'I wouldn't have shot anyone. It wasn't a real gun!'

O'Yee turned to look at the pistol. The fall had snapped it in half and there was a roll of toy caps sticking out of its muzzle near a collection of brittle plastic and metal springs.

'All right,' O'Yee said. 'We don't kill people here. We arrest them.'

The Negro released a sigh of relief. He said, 'I'm scared of guns.'

'Gun?' O'Yee said to himself. He thought, 'Gun?' He said, 'Shit! *Gun!*'

He knew he had forgotten something.

Mrs Skilbeck said, 'No.' She waved Auden aside. She said, 'I'm not talking to any of you unhelpful bastards and I'm not letting you go away for hours to talk to that Chinese girl. I'm going through to talk to that Chinese girl.'

And she did.

'Not bad,' the manager said. He watched the police van until it disappeared around the corner, 'It's a pity it wasn't more dramatic.' He said it to the accompaniment of a burst of machine gun fire from inside the theatre, 'Still, you got him.'

'I got him,' O'Yee said. He glanced under his coat to make sure he had remembered to put his pistol back in the shoulder holster, 'I didn't have to fire a shot.'

The manager stepped back a pace and swelled his chest. 'On behalf of the principals of this beautiful cinema and to show our esteem and gratitude for the service you have performed on behalf of the police force of this city, as the manager of this beautiful cinema theatre I have been asked by my principals to hand to you this small token of our appreciation and esteem with the best wishes of the staff and principals and management of the Peacock Cinema, Hong Bay, British Crown

Colony of Hong Kong. Presented to Detective Inspector O'Yee by Mr Oswald Han.' He tapped his coat lightly with his thumb, 'That's me.'

'Thank you, Mr Han,' O'Yee said, 'but we're not allowed to take money.'

A look of horror flitted across Mr Han's features. 'It isn't *money*!' What a suggestion—

'Thanks,' O'Yee said. Mr Han handed him a sealed envelope. O'Yee said, 'I'll open it in the presence of witnesses at the Police Station.'

'It isn't money,' Mr Han said again. 'It certainly isn't money.'

It wasn't. It was a year's free admission pass to the afternoon and morning sessions at the Peacock Cinema, Icehouse Street, Hong Bay, presented to Mr O'Yee by Mr Oswald Han, Manager—front stalls.

'No,' Minnie Oh said, 'he hasn't.'

'Aren't you going to look for him?'

'There's not a great deal we can do,' Minnie said. She moved the stack of handout sheets warning whores about the dangers of VD without a regular checkup out of Mrs Skilbeck's view. It was in Cantonese, but there were some graphic illustrations. 'He's only been missing a few hours. Have you tried the airport? Perhaps he's gone back there. There hasn't been an accident or we would have heard about it. Perhaps he's—'

'Perhaps he's in jail!' Mrs Skilbeck said bitterly, 'I'll kill him.'

'No,' Minnie Oh said. She smiled pleasantly and shook her head to show just how far removed the residents of Yellowthread Street's jail were from respectable American tourists from New Jersey. 'The only people in jail here at the moment are an axe murderer and someone who won't give his name who assaulted a policeman.'

'They don't sound like my husband,' Mrs Skilbeck said. She rose, and sniffed at the VD brochures. She said, 'You don't have a very nice job for a young girl.'

'No,' Minnie said.

'I'll be back,' Mrs Skilbeck said, and left.

At midnight Hot Time Alice decided that business at *Alice's* could take care of itself while she went around to *Alice's Goldsmith's and Jewellery* to check that the customer-deterring fingers on the display cases had been removed by the ambulancemen.

She waddled into the store at exactly seven minutes past midnight, found the assistant smoking a cigarette, roared at him, sat down behind the counter with her books and her cashbox and sent him out to bring her back a bottle of beer.

At eight minutes past midnight the Mongolian came in. He examined Alice (Alice examined him), decided she was the cleaning woman pilfering cash from the fingerless proprietor (Alice decided he was no customer), and said, 'Owner!'

'I'm the owner,' Alice said. She shut the metal cashbox and stood up with her fat hands on her hips.

'Owner,' the Mongolian said. He was not a man to entertain two thoughts in his shaven head at the same time, 'Owner!'

People didn't talk to Alice in that tone. 'People don't talk to me in that tone,' Alice said. 'So get out!'

'Owner,' the Mongolian said.

'Me!' Alice said. She flicked her thumb at her giant breasts, 'Owner—me!'

'Police,' the Mongolian said.

'Like hell you are,' Alice said.

'You police.'

'Like hell I am.'

The Mongolian shook his head. 'No call police.'

Alice leaned back on the heels of her shoes and gave the impression of looking down from her five foot three to the Mongolian's lesser six foot three.

The Mongolian thumped his barrel-stave chest with his

thumb. It sounded like an elephant's heart beating at full charge. 'Mongolian,' the Mongolian said.

Hot Time Alice Ping stopped leaning back on the heels of her shoes.

'No police,' the Mongolian said. 'No police.'

Alice put her fingers behind her back, still attached to her wrists and going to stay that way.

'Fingers,' the Mongolian said.

'We can talk about this,' Alice said, 'Listen, we can talk about—'

'No police. Bad thing,' the Mongolian, who was no good at long conversations, said. He drew his eleven-inch-long knife and lopped at Alice's ear which she did not have behind her back.

There were then a number of sounds in the store in Camphorwood Lane. There was a swish as the kukri completed its arc and a click as the Mongolian sheathed it in the same motion, a metallic tinkle as Alice's bangle earring struck the glass counter, a plop as Alice's ear followed it, the sound of the Mongolian's footsteps on the floor as he left, a clunk as he shut the glass door behind him, and finally, Alice's broken voice as she began running about in tiny circles behind the counter looking at her ear and screaming.

The assistant came back with the beer, looked at the ear and the glass counter, at Hot Time Alice Ping running, and drank the contents of the bottle in one gulp.

A.M.

There were two conferences going on in Hong Bay. It was two fifteen in the morning and at the venue of the first conference, the Yellowthread Street Police Station, the atmosphere was stale and fuggy with cigarette smoke, half empty cardboard cups of aromatic burnt-bean coffee, O'Yee's almost devoured night meal of take-away noodles and pork, and Auden's and O'Yee's bad jokes.

'Ear today, gone tomorrow,' O'Yee said and popped noodles into his mouth.

Feiffer continued reading Spencer's report on his first interview with Hot Time Alice Ping of the two ears and Sister Sung's telephoned news of Hot Time Alice Ping of the one. Feiffer said, 'Shut up.'

'Don't be so cruel,' Spencer said to O'Yee and Auden. He read his report over Feiffer's shoulder.

'Ear's to you,' O'Yee said and raised his cup.

Auden collapsed in helpless laughter and banged his desk.

'The Andrews Sisters,' Feiffer said. He said to Spencer, 'What's this word?'

'Frank,' Spencer said. He read on, '... it was a frank and meaningful interview ...'

'It says "frunk".'

'It's the typewriter,' Spencer said.

Auden banged on his desk.

Two streets away, in *Alice's*, the customers had been cleared out and the place closed for a private party (the notice on the door said). The guests had come down from Hanford Hill and they were not feeling very festive. Mr Boon had come down from the hill and he never felt festive. Tonight he was downright peeved. Mr Boon looked at Alice. Alice sat opposite him in a wheelchair with her ear wrapped in a space helmet bandage. Mr Boon sucked his hollow tooth and felt peeved. He sucked his hollow tooth again. Mr Boon turned his head to another angle and looked at Alice out of the corner of his eye and sucked his hollow tooth.

'All my friends,' Alice said sentimentally. The men from Hanford Hill, their bodyguards, their employees and Alice sat in a circle in the middle of the cleared dance floor and ashed their cigarettes into a centrally placed brass spittoon; 'My dear old friends,' Alice said and wiped a jelly tear from her mummy-wrapped cheek. 'My dear, dear old friends,' Alice said.

Mr Boon moved his head and contemplated Alice from under hooded lids. 'Quiet, woman,' Mr Boon said.

'Yes, Mr Boon,' Alice said.

Mr Boon sucked his hollow tooth again. Mr Boon was in his late fifties, fat and well oiled, well preserved and looked after; he had an almost full set of gold-filled dentures, but he had a hollow tooth. He sucked it.

'Mongolian,' Mr Boon said, 'Mongolian.'

'Independent,' Hernando Haw from Macao said. He curled his lip, 'Independent.'

'Hmm,' Mr Boon said. He blew a pollution of smoke into the circle like the Queen Elizabeth with its boilers shut down. Outside the circle, against the walls, the whores stood at various points of the compass watching the men and the smoke and the toothsucking like a scene from *The Hustler*. 'Low Fat?' Mr Boon said.

'Independent operator,' Low Fat said. He shook his head. 'Independent.'

'Stupid,' Mr Boon said.

'Stupid,' Hernando Haw from Macao agreed.

Low Fat bobbed his head up and down. 'Stupid.'

Mr Boon surveyed the antidotes to stupidity in his dance hall pharmacy. He looked at Shotgun Sen. He looked at The Club (With Nails). He looked at Osaka Onuki the Disemboweller. He looked at Crushed Toes and the other one (no one knew his name—he was The Fourth Gangster) and he thought them a potent bunch.

'Stupid,' Mr Boon said. He waved his hand in deep pity for someone so stupid. 'So, so sad, sad stupid.'

'Stupid!' Mr Boon said. *'Stupid!'*

Mr Haw from Macao nodded, Low Fat nodded, Alice nodded, the henchmen nodded, Osaka Onuki the Disemboweller ran his thumb along the hone of the short sword under his coat and he nodded. Apricot Tang Lee shot a thrilled look at Posey Yin and Tinkerbell Lin Wong and she nodded.

Alice said, 'Stupid.'

Mr Boon turned his attention to Osaku Onuki. He considered the little Japanese's squat body and the ripple of his shoulders and forearms under his little squat Japanese suit. Osaka Onuki giggled and touched at his short sword.

'Kukri,' Mr Boon said, 'Indian Gurkha knife one foot long, very sharp.'

Osaka Onuki the Disemboweller giggled. Mr Boon turned his eyes on to Shotgun Sen. The twin barrels of Sen's sawed-off twelve-gauge shotgun under his left armpit down to his trouser belt made him look like a fat frog with goitre. Shotgun Sen patted the outline of the twin barrels. Crushed Toes said nothing. He tapped the base of his chair with a fast rhythmic tapping and waited for Mr Boon to give the word. The Fourth Gangster crossed his arms and touched at the two pistols in shoulder holsters he wore, one under each armpit, and made a kissing sound at the floor. Apricot Tang Lee felt a shiver of excitement run up her back and down into her underwear.

'Warn, hurt, cripple, kill,' Mr Haw from Macao said. They were the choices to be voted on, 'Blind, amputate, scar, castrate.'

'Kill!' Alice said through her swathes of linen.

Mr Boon thought about it. He sucked his hollow tooth in contemplation.

Francis John Vinehouse, aged fifty, was the Hong Bay taxman. He went into the bar Feiffer had gone into earlier in the day and sat down. A stripper was in the process of removing her bra from her breasts and he waited until, released, they bobbed up and down like two ripe melons to the bumping of the music from a scratched record on a player on the bar. Then he took out a little leather covered notebook and made an entry in it with his Parker pen.

Entertainment tax not paid, he wrote in the notebook. He wrote the date and put the word *Entertainment* after it. He counted the audience of happy drinkers and wrote *Audience: 37.*

He glanced at the stripper. She had blotches on her stomach and acne on her face.

Mr Vinehouse was a regulation man. If the tax regulations considered it entertainment, it was entertainment, and if Mr Vinehouse himself did not consider it entertainment and the regulations did Mr Vinehouse admitted his error. It was entertainment.

He underlined the word in his little leather covered notebook—*Entertainment*—and put the Parker pen back carefully into his shirt pocket.

'Four fingers and one ear,' Feiffer said. He put the reports down on his desk and lit a cigarette, 'Our Mongolian friend runs a busy trade. Have we got any leads on him?'

O'Yee shook his head.

'Nothing known? No previous?'

O'Yee shook his head.

'An independent?'

O'Yee nodded.

Spencer glared at O'Yee. It was Spencer's case, Spencer

thought. He said, 'Alice said he was new.'

'Christopher—' Feiffer began. O'Yee yawned and grasped his heart. He said in great pain and discomfort, 'Oh—!'

'The old trouble again?' Feiffer enquired pleasantly.

'The old trouble,' O'Yee said. He nodded bravely, 'I've done my bit for the night.'

'He's pretending,' Spencer said. He looked at O'Yee with contempt. 'He's just pretending so he can get out of doing anything about it. It's my case anyway.'

'Right!' O'Yee said readily. He nodded encouragingly to Feiffer, 'It's his case. He got it all out of Alice.'

'I did,' Spencer said. 'It was a very valuable interview.'

'Keen as mustard,' O'Yee said. He broke into what he thought was his *Destry Rides Again* voice, 'Give the kid a break, Sheriff.'

'Auden?'

'I've got an accident report to type up, Boss,' Auden said. He held the particular piece of paper above his head and screwed it quickly into his typewriter, 'See?'

'I've done my bit for the night too,' Feiffer said, 'I'm not going to stand out in Camphorwood Lane for the rest of the night dying for a pee in case some mad bastard with a kukri turns up.'

'Quite right,' O'Yee said. 'You have to think of your wife and children.'

'He hasn't got any children,' Spencer said irritably. He couldn't understand it. It was typical: because Alice had a bad reputation everyone was against her. He said, 'If you're all so afraid why don't you send little Minnie Oh to do your work for you?'

'Good idea,' O'Yee said. 'That's a very good idea.'

'You stink!' Spencer said, 'Poor Alice Ping.'

'Poor One-Eared Alice Ping,' O'Yee said, 'Poor Hot Time One-Eared Frank and Valuable Alice.' He said, 'I've done my bit for law and order.'

Feiffer decided.

'We'll leave it till the morning,' Feiffer said. 'The day shift can handle it. He won't do anything else tonight. I think I'm right.'

He wasn't. He was wrong. At that exact moment, the Mongolian was having a short but communicative discussion with Mr Edgar Tan of *Edgar Tan and Company, Jewellers,* two doors away from *Alice's Goldsmith's and Jewellery.*

It was an extremely brief discussion.

The Mongolian said, 'Money,' and Mr Edgar Tan broke into laughter.

The Mongolian said, 'Money,' and drew his kukri and Mr Edgar Tan said, 'Ha-ha!'

The Mongolian said, 'Fingers,' and Mr Tan danced away and said, 'You in big trouble.'

'Money!' the Mongolian repeated. Mr Tan repeated, 'Ha!' The Mongolian ordered, 'Hand!'

'You in big trouble,' Mr Tan said, 'Wrong person to chop. Hanford Hill gang.' He stood out of range and waggled his still intact index finger, 'Wrong, wrong, wrong, Hanford Hill —wrong, wrong, wrong.'

'Money!' the Mongolian said. He kicked aside one of the counter display cases and faced the waggling finger. The finger disappeared behind its owner's back. 'Wrong, wrong, wrong,' Mr Tan chided him, 'Wrong, wrong, wrong.'

The Mongolian looked at Mr Tan. Mr Tan smiled happily. The Mongolian looked at his eleven-inch long kukri with a silver lion's head pommel. 'Wrong—ha!' Mr Tan said. 'Can do nothing—wrong, wrong, wrong.'

So the Mongolian killed him.

'Hernando?' Mr Boon asked.

Hernando Haw from Macao shook his head, 'Cripple.'

'No!' Alice protested. Mr Boon ignored her.

'Cripple,' Mr Boon confirmed, 'Cripple?'

'Cripple,' Mr Haw said. He threw his extinct cheroot butt

into the brass spittoon. Crushed Toes grinned lovingly at him. Crushed Toes was the official crippler.

'Low?' Mr Boon asked.

Low Fat considered it. He said, 'I don't know ...'

Crushed Toes nodded encouragingly at him. Low Fat looked at Tinkerbell Lin Wong. 'I don't know what Miss Alice wants.' He looked pointedly at Tinkerbell Lin Wong.

'Kill!' One-Eared Alice said, 'Kill!' She touched at her ear bandages gingerly, 'Look what that bastard did to me!'

'Hmm,' Mr Boon said. He said kindly to Low, 'Take your time; no one wants to make the wrong decision.'

Hernando Haw made a tiny bow of respect to Low Fat. He said, 'It's all right with me. I don't mind.' He explained with a little self critical motion of his chin: 'I'm always a little over cautious.'

'That's very often a good trait to have,' Low Fat said chivalrously, 'you shouldn't be embarrassed.'

'Thank you,' Hernando Haw said. 'I call it subtlety.'

'Quite right,' Mr Low said. He caught Tinkerbell Lin Wong's eyes looking at him, 'Still, a man does have to be violent on occasion. A man has to have the thrusting fierceness of white steel.'

'Hmm,' Mr Boon said, 'take your time.'

'Look!' Alice said suddenly. She tapped her bandages hard. It hurt. 'Look at what he did to me!'

'Poor old Alice,' Spencer said. He fixed his attention on to the line in Chen's statement form that said *Witness To Statement* .... *Rank* .... *Number* .... and signed through a gauze curtain of hot tears. 'Poor old Alice,' he said bitterly.

'Quite right,' O'Yee said, 'The day shift will be righteously diligent.'

'Oh, shut up,' Spencer said. He was the newest member of the Station and he thought they were picking on him. 'Oh, shut up,' Spencer said. He thought he had been so forthright and firm and policeman-ish at *Alice's*. 'Oh, shut up,' Spencer said again.

'Who's doing all the talking?' O'Yee asked. He began to type out the circumstances of the Negro's arrest and found that any way he put it made him sound like a cross between Dick Tracy and the Lone Ranger. He said, 'Jesus, this is going to look good on my record, this one,' and ignored Spencer's barely audible rejoinder of 'Oh, shut up.'

The barman came over to Francis John Vinehouse the taxman as the fat stripper's fat legs wobbled her off to the makeshift dressing room behind a curtain to put clothes on again so she could take them off.

'Mr Lop,' Mr Vinehouse greeted him.

'Hullo,' Mr Lop said. He sat down at the table unhappily, 'More trouble?'

'Not for me,' Mr Vinehouse said. 'For you.'

'Your Cantonese is getting better,' Mr Lop said morosely. 'Do you want to talk in English?'

'No,' Mr Vinehouse said. There was an opened bottle of Tiger beer on the table in front of him. He slid it towards Mr Lop.

'Aren't you going to drink it?' Mr Lop asked without interest. 'You're going to claim it on expenses so you might as well drink it.'

Mr Vinehouse shook his head. The Department did not encourage intemperance.

Mr Lop shrugged. He took up the bottle and drained it. He said, 'Tell me the bad news.'

Mr Vinehouse touched at the glass beside the empty bottle. Glasses were to drink things out of. 'Entertainment,' Mr Vinehouse said.

Mr Lop turned the bottle upside down and watched the last drops of beer dribble out on to the table. He jerked his head to where the customers sat in hushed silence watching the silhouette of the stripper dressing behind the threadbare curtain. 'That?' Mr Lop asked with distaste.

'Entertainment,' Mr Vinehouse said.

'Do you think so?'

'Your customers think so.'

Mr Lop sniffed. He owned a place like this, he worked in a place like this, he drew his sustenance and the food for his children's mouths from a place like this, but that didn't mean he had to be lacking in taste. 'No,' Mr Lop said.

'Yes,' Mr Vinehouse said, 'and you haven't paid your tax on it.'

'Entertainment tax?'

'You haven't registered it, you haven't advised the Department of it, you haven't made a note of it in your interim statement, and you haven't paid it.'

'O.K.,' Mr Lop said, 'I'll pay it.'

'When?'

'Well—' Mr Lop said. He ran through a directory of possible dates, months and years in his mind. 'Next.'

'Next what?'

'Next time.'

'Now,' Mr Vinehouse said. He noticed the stripper finish dressing so she could undress and the assistant barman cock the stylus arm on the plastic covered record player on the bar. 'Now would be best,' Mr Vinehouse said.

'Hoh!' Mr Lop said. He raised his arms and his eyes to Heaven at the suggestion, 'If only that were possible—hoh!' He shook his head as the unutterably sad truth about his finances and the health of his children and the temper of his wife and the infirmity of his aged parents swept over him under his mask of host and bon vivant to the world, 'Hoh!' Mr Lop said, 'If only you knew—'

'Arseholes,' Mr Vinehouse said quietly. The music recommenced and the dancer brought her fat body out in front of the curtain.

'Hoh!' the barman said, a figure of abject tragedy and the aproned repository of the world's woes, 'Hoh!'

Mr Vinehouse waited.

Mr Low looked at Tinkerbell Lin Wong. He liked his people intact. He said to Mr Boon, 'Whatever you decide.'

The phone rang on the wall near the bar.

Alice said, 'Look at what he—' but Mr Boon raised his hand to silence her and jerked his head at The Fourth Gangster to answer the telephone.

Edgar Tan's assistant was named Tommy Lai and he was put out. One of the display counters had been smashed, rings, earrings, cufflinks and assorted items of value lay on the floor covered in blood, Mr Tan lay on the floor covered in blood, there was blood on Tommy Lai's shoes and in his socks, the policeman knelt down by Mr Tan's body with blood on the knees of his khaki trousers, there was blood on the walls, and the policeman wanted to use the telephone.

The policeman stood up from Mr Tan's blood and said, 'Hurry up with the phone.'

'It's ringing,' Tommy Lai said, 'I can't make it go any faster.'

Constable Cho said, 'This is murder, I want to use the phone.' A herd of sightseers crowded at the open door and in front of the glass windows. Constable Cho said, 'I'm going to clear the doorway and then I want the phone.'

At the other end of the line, the telephone stopped buzzing. 'Hullo!' Tommy said urgently.

'Yeah?'

'Tommy Lai.'

'Who?'

'Lai, Tommy, *Edgar*—' —maybe, he thought, he should have said 'The late'—'*Edgar Tan and Company, Jewellers.*'

'So what?' the voice said.

'Tommy *Lai*. They said at the house that I had to ring your number'—Constable Cho was moving the crowd away from the doorway and the window—'Tell whoever's there that it's Tommy Lai.'

'O.K.,' the voice said. The voice said into an abyss, 'Tommy Lai—' and then put the phone down on a table or a chair.

'Speak,' another voice said.

Constable Cho came back into the blood shop. 'Phone.' He came forward to take it.

'Speak quickly,' the voice said.

Tommy spoke.

The stripper stripped, then went back behind the curtain to dress again.

'Feiffer,' the barman said.

'What?'

'Feiffer,' Mr Lop said, 'Inspector Feiffer sent you to get me.'

'Who's Inspector Feiffer?'

Mr Lop shook his head sadly. The world was a place of unending and bitter disappointments. 'After all we did for him.' He shook his head sadly, 'What a comment on the European mind.'

'Tax,' Mr Vinehouse said, 'We got the word from the Licensing Office that this area was going to be blitzed. We work all night at the tax office these days catching up with people like you.' It was a thankless task.

'Feiffer,' Mr Lop said sadly. 'After all we did. We saved his life, you know. There was a madman with a knife after him.'

'I don't know any Feiffer,' Mr Vinehouse said. 'Tax. Or I'll have the police close the place down.'

'Ah,' Mr Lop said. They would too, led by Feiffer. 'Ah,' Mr Lop said. He went over to the bar and started the record player music so that he would not hear his pen scratching on the cheque.

'Ah,' Mr Lop said to his departing bank balance, 'Ah ...'

The stripper came out from behind the threadbare curtain, half dressed and cursing.

Mr Lop thought he would never help a cop again.

'Mr Boon ...' Alice said entreatingly. She touched at her ear absence with lost love. She opened her hand to him in supplication, 'Mr Boon ...' She leaned forward to crave his grace, 'Mr Boon ...'

Low Fat looked hungrily at Tinkerbell Lin Wong.

Mr Boon lit a cigarette and looked at the inanimate telephone on the wall.

'It's a matter of considering the profit in actions,' subtle Hernando Haw from Macao began to explain to Alice and the gang. 'To rush blindly in like madmen is not to consider that each action in life is intimately intermeshed with considerations of business and profitable dealing. To consider each and every action carefully and in advance is the sign of a—'

'Kill,' Mr Boon said.

'Of course,' Hernando Haw said, 'Killing would be best.'

'Kill,' Mr Boon said.

'If you like,' Low Fat said. 'Anything you decide is O.K. with me.'

Mr Boon kept his eyes on the telephone. He said, 'Kill.'

Alice drew in her breath and turned herself into a pregnant pigeon. She ruffled her feathers happily and tapped at the ear bandages girlishly with his shoulder. She said, 'Dee-dum,' lightly and merrily and tapped at her ear.

'Kill,' Mr Boon said.

'Kill,' Hernando Haw said. 'Kill the Mongolian bastard.'

'Mongolian bastard,' Low Fat said. Tinkerbell Lin Wong smiled at him secretly and he smiled back secretly at Tinkerbell Lin Wong.

'My friends,' Alice said.

'My friend,' Low Fat said to Tinkerbell Lin Wong.

'My agreement,' Hernando Haw said. He indicated that section of the seated lethal human flesh that was his. He offered it to Mr Boon's disposition. Hernando Haw said, 'My personnel.'

'Edgar Tan and Company,' Mr Boon said.

'My dear friends,' Alice said.

'Yes?' Hernando Haw said to Mr Boon.

'My shop,' Mr Boon said, 'That Mongolian bastard's dead. That was my shop!'

'My God!' The Club (With Nails) who was a failed Presbyterian said.

'—my revenge—!' Alice protested.

'My shop!' Mr Boon said and sucked his hollow tooth. He sent The Fourth Gangster out to another of his bars across the road to get more men.

Spencer was on the phone. He said unhappily, 'Yellowthread Street—yes, Constable Cho?'

Spencer said, 'Really? Gosh!'

O'Yee glanced at him. Ah Pin the cleaner came hobbling in the front door to begin his early morning sweeping. O'Yee said to him in English, 'Hullo, Ah Pin.'

'Inspector sir,' Ah Pin said.

'What do you hear, Pin?' Feiffer asked absently. He lifted the statement form off Spencer's desk and checked that it was properly signed, 'How's life?'

Ah Pin opened the door of the broom closet behind the main door and took out the tools of his trade.

'Go on,' Spencer said into the phone. He was scribbling details of the call on his desk blotter, 'I'm taking it all down.'

'See Miss Oh in Icehouse Street,' Ah Pin told no one in particular. 'No good place for lady policeman.'

'She must have gone out the back way,' Auden commented bitterly to O'Yee.

'Devious,' O'Yee said, 'more VD notices for the girlies.'

'See her near Jasmine Steps going Wanchai Street,' Ah Pin said.

'Who the bloody hell typed up this statement form?' Feiffer demanded, 'It's bloody illegible. What the hell does "contession" mean?' He took out his pen and changed it to 'confession'.

'Spencer,' Auden said.

'Auden,' O'Yee said.

'She go about killing?' Ah Pin asked. He swept away two empty coffee cups and a ragged trail of cigarette butts into a cut-open one gallon tin made into a dustpan.

Feiffer said, 'I'm going to type these things myself in future. I do all the work and this is what I get to show for it.' He glanced hungrily at O'Yee's machine, 'Does your typewriter work, Christopher?'

'No,' O'Yee said. 'Keep your lustful eyes off my typewriter and use your own.'

'Mine needs repair or someone around here needs typing lessons.' He said to Ah Pin, 'What killing? Oh, no. That's all sorted out.'

'You get him?' Ah Pin asked happily. It was nice to be associated with the workings of justice. Policemen were nice to know: they gave you a feeling of security and armed might.

'Yeah,' Feiffer said, 'he's in the cells.'

'What name?'

Feiffer considered the illiteracy of Inspectors and the generally debilitating effect working in Hong Bay had on the English language. 'Can't tell you that,' he said to Pin. 'Not allowed. You know that. Don't ask.'

'Go on,' Spencer said hoarsely into the phone. His breathing came more heavily and he wiped a bead of sweat away from under his eyes.

O'Yee looked up at the ceiling fan. It was working. He said to Auden, 'He must be talking to Sweaty Glance Minnie Oh. Either that or it's the old white man's burden of constipation again.'

'Go on,' Spencer said excitedly into the phone.

'Bad man,' Pin said to the floor, 'bad man Mongolian man.'

'Hmm,' Feiffer said.

'Bad killing.'

'Who?'

'Man being killed Camphorwood Lane,' Ah Pin said as to an idiot boy, 'bad, bad.'

'What?' Feiffer said. 'Who's being killed?'

'Killing all over finish now,' Pin said. He was, Feiffer had reckoned once in an idle moment, no less than eighty summers ancient, and he had one arm grown longer than the other from permanently pushing a broom across police station floors. Ah Pin said, 'You get him quick. Good in cell.'

'Who?' Feiffer asked. He felt like an idiot boy.

'Go on,' Spencer said, but whoever it was at the other end of the telephone must have said, 'That's all.' Spencer said, 'Oh—'

'Mongolian kill Edgar Tan in Camphorwood Lane,' Ah Pin said. 'He kill him bang! bang! chop! chop! dead.'

Spencer hung up the phone. He paused. He regarded Feiffer with a look of secret triumph. He regarded Auden as a failed rival. He regarded O'Yee with undisguised contempt. He said, 'You'll never guess—'

'I'll be buggered!' Feiffer said. He said to Spencer, 'The Mongolian's killed Edgar Tan in Camphorwood Lane.'

Spencer looked at him. His mouth fell open. He said, 'I know!'

Feiffer looked at him. He shook his head at Spencer's moronically fallen open countenance. Feiffer said, 'Why the bloody hell didn't you tell us?' He said, 'My God, you must be deranged!'

Mrs Skilbeck tipped the bellboy insultingly inadequately and pulled her mouth back over her teeth. She looked at the seven suitcases on the double bed and felt her fury increase. The bellboy cleared his throat uncomfortably and pulled the door to quickly. She was bigger than he was.

Mrs Skilbeck lit a cigarette, looked at the luggage, sucked the life out of the cigarette, smashed it into a glass ashtray on the dresser and felt furious.

The airline label attached to the top suitcase said in gay Italic script, *Sorry! But we got it back for you and we're sorry. Honest!*

Mrs Skilbeck ripped the label off the handle and stamped her foot on it.

She said aloud, 'I'm going to kill him!' and stamped on the label again. She lit another cigarette, gathered up her raffia bag, went out, and slammed the door behind her so hard the key fell out. She picked it up and stuffed it into her raffia bag and thought she wasn't going to hand the key into some goddamned hotel clerk so he could lose it the way everything got lost around here.

Mrs Skilbeck was furious.

O'Yee's phone rang. The voice, a drunken voice, said, 'Feiffer!'

O'Yee handed the phone to Feiffer. He said, 'It's your wife.'

'Hullo?' Feiffer said pleasantly.

'This is an anonymous call,' the drunken man's voice said, 'I'm going to get you!'

'How are you, darling?'

'Feiffer?'

'That's right.'

'This is a—'

'O.K.'

'I'm going to get you!'

'Goodbye, dear,' Feiffer said. He hung up.

'Who was it?' O'Yee asked. They had been questioning Ah Pin. O'Yee forgot what he was going to ask. He said again, 'Who was it?'

'Where did you hear about this killing?' Feiffer asked Ah Pin. 'Who told you?'

'I hear.'

'Where from?'

'Who was it?' O'Yee asked again.

'Who told you?'

Ah Pin put down his broom. He glanced at the clock. Time spent talking to policemen was time not spent brooming. He rested his elbow on Feiffer's desk and thought about it.

'Well?' Feiffer asked.

'Don't you think we ought to—' Spencer said. He wanted to get out and solve the crime.

'Cho's there,' Feiffer told him. 'The body isn't going anywhere.' He watched Ah Pin think. It was a painful sight to see. He asked Ah Pin, 'Well?'

'It wasn't your wife,' O'Yee said, 'It was a drunken man. I only said it was your wife—'

'Cousin,' Ah Pin said. 'Cousin tell me.'

'Where?'

'Camphorwood Lane.'

'What were you doing in Camphorwood Lane?'

'Not me; killing in Camphorwood Lane. Ah Pin not in—'

'Did your cousin see it happen?'

Ah Pin thought about it. He shook his head.

'It was a joke!' O'Yee said desperately, 'It was a bad joke! It wasn't your wife at all!'

'Cousin tell me in Icehouse Street.'

'Where in Icehouse Street?'

Ah Pin was a friend of the police. Without them, food would stop. Life had to go on. He said, 'Cousin say Tan shop man killed. Big trouble. Shop of Mr Boon.'

'Aye?' O'Yee said. He forgot about the mystery of the drunken transvestite wife with the deep voice, 'What did you say?' He said in Cantonese, 'What did you say?'

'Mr Boon's shop,' Ah Pin said back in Cantonese. He thought O'Yee spoke it quite well for a half-Chinese, better than Feiffer or the others, in fact, reasonably well. He said totally ungrammatically, 'Gangster Boon shop of Hanford Hill.'

'Jesus,' Auden said.

Spencer said, 'Gosh!'

'This man Tan was an employee of Mr Boon's? Is that what you're saying?'

'Yes.'

Feiffer looked at Ah Pin's eighty ancient summers. He said,

'How does your cousin know that?'

'Cousin gangster,' Ah Pin said proudly. 'Work for Mr Boon.'

The phone on O'Yee's desk rang again. O'Yee looked at it. He waived its sole rights to Feiffer with a motion of his hand.

'What?' Feiffer said into the phone.

'Feiffer?' the drunken voice demanded, 'Listen, I'm going to get you!'

Feiffer hung up. 'Where did you see your cousin?' he asked Pin.

'Icehouse Street. See Miss Oh in Icehouse Street near Jasmine Steps. Big gangster talk about Mongolian bastard. Going kill Mongolian bastard bang! bang! chop! chop! dead.'

'Constable Oh's gone down to the dancehall district,' Feiffer said.

'Yes.'

'What do you mean, "yes"?'

'Gangsters in dancehall district bang! bang!—'

'Where?' Feiffer demanded, 'You saw Boon and—'

'No saw—Mr Boon, Macao man, Low Fat going to—'

'Bang, bang, chop, chop,' Spencer said nervously. He thought of fragile Minnie Oh in the middle of a Saint Valentine's Day shoot-out and his heart sank.

'Yes!' Ah Pin said gleefully. If you told them enough times eventually they got it, 'Yes! Yes!'

The phone rang again. Feiffer lifted it off the cradle and then replaced it.

'Where's the Mongolian now?'

'Not know,' Ah Pin admitted regretfully. He brightened up. 'No one know. Police not know. Gangsters not know.' He smiled widely, 'No one know.' He nodded to himself sagely, 'Clever fellow Mongolian.' No one said anything else to him so he went back to his sweeping.

'Mongolian,' Mr Boon said to the circle. He was met by blank stares and slowly shaken heads, 'The Mongolian lives—where?'

'He's an independent,' Alice said. They were the difficult ones to find. Low Fat smiled at Tinkerbell Lin Wong and considered her young body.

'Hmm,' Mr Boon said. He gazed at the flesh of Apricot Tang Lee, Posey Yin and Tinkerbell Lin Wong with the knowledge of the human foibles such flesh aroused. He said, 'Your girls know where he lives.'

'No,' Alice Ping said. 'I'm like their mother. They would have told me.' She said to the girls, 'You would have told Mummy.'

Mr Boon glanced at her with a glance of brief nausea. He asked the girls brusquely, 'Which one of you works Camphorwood Lane?'

'No!' Alice said, 'My girls work for me. I've given them a roof over their heads. They don't work the lanes any more.'

'Dung!' Mr Boon said. He said, 'Which one works Camphorwood Lane?'

No one answered.

'Five hundred dollars,' Mr Boon said, 'for the one who tells me which one. Face acid for the one who works Camphorwood Lane and lies.'

Tinkerbell Lin Wong worked Camphorwood Lane on her days off. She knew the Mongolian. She knew where he lived. Posey Yin said, 'Her.'

'You,' Mr Boon said. Low Fat looked surprised.

Low Fat said, 'You?'

'Her,' Posey Yin said.

'You—' Alice Ping started, but Mr Boon said, 'You.' He fixed Tinkerbell with his unblinking eyes, 'Mongolian lives —where?'

'Roof,' Tinkerbell Lin Wong said. She was not one to compound her errors. 'Roof opposite shop of Edgar Tan.' She smiled nervously at Low Fat. Low Fat pursed his lips and considered this new complication to his otherwise uncomplicated life.

'Acid in the face . . .' Alice said unhappily. She touched her ear and tut-tutted. She said again, 'Acid in the face ... tsk, tsk.'

'Got protector,' Tinkerbell said. She glanced at Low Fat and nodded. She said spitefully to Alice, 'Got big man protector.'

'Who?' Mr Boon asked Low Fat.

'Beats me,' Low Fat said. He shook his head at Tinkerbell Lin Wong in dismay and incomprehension. He went out to the cars with the others.

Low Fat thought of himself as many things. Other people thought of him as many things. Suicidal, however, was not one of them.

The phone rang again. Feiffer picked it up and said, 'Stuff off!'

It was Minnie Oh.

Feiffer said, 'Oh—'

'Yes,' Minnie said, 'it's me.'

'Oh,' Feiffer said.

'Yes,' Minnie said again. She thought something terrible must have happened at the station for Feiffer to have become unhinged. She said, 'I'm across from *Alice's*.'

'You'd better get out of there,' Feiffer said, 'Boon and his gang are down from the Hill and they're somewhere in that area.'

'I know,' Minnie's voice said, 'I can see them across the street. They're all coming out of *Alice's* and getting into cars. One of them has a shotgun under his coat.'

'Right,' Feiffer said.

'They're getting into five cars, all black Fords'—she read off the licence plate numbers—'I counted eight or nine of them.' There was a pause. Feiffer could hear the traffic going past in the street and the voices of two men bartering over the price of a tailoring job in the shop Minnie was evidently ringing from. Then there was the sound of a tram going past.

'Minnie?' Feiffer said into the noise of the tram, 'Minnie?'

The tram went past. 'Minnie?'

'What's the matter?' Auden said urgently.

'Minnie's seen Boon and his friends.' He said again into the phone, 'Minnie? Damn it, answer!'

'Oh, no ...' Spencer said to himself quietly. He said forebodingly, 'Oh, no ...'

O'Yee watched Feiffer. He said to Spencer, 'She can take care of herself.' He said to Feiffer, 'Harry?'

Feiffer shook his head. 'She just went off the—'

'Inspector Feiffer?' Minnie's voice asked.

'Yes. Where the hell were—'

'I went into the street to see where they went.' She paused. She said, 'The three lead cars went up Icehouse Street and turned right.' She dropped her voice and added urgently, 'They're coming up Yellowthread Street. They should pass you any minute.'

'Right,' Feiffer said. He said, 'You get the hell up here as fast as you can and don't come near anyone until you get in the back door and draw yourself a weapon.' He hung up and said to the others as one, 'They're coming up the street. Out!'

Spencer looked at him.

'Everyone,' Feiffer said. He drew his pistol and stuck it more accessibly in the waistband of his trousers.

Auden took his Colt Python from its desk drawer and checked it.

The telephone rang shrilly on Feiffer's desk. He picked it up quickly.

The drunk said, 'Now listen, Feiffer—' Feiffer hung up.

'O.K.,' he said to the detectives, 'No bloody shooting, but I want the one with the shotgun.'

Spencer made it to the door before any of them.

The Government Medical Examiner was a tall, fair-haired Aryan type with a Roman nose who chain-smoked French cigarettes. With him bending over the body of the dead Mr Tan, a Hong Kong Chinese corpse of Taiwanese extraction, it was like a minor meeting of the United Nations.

'Doctor?' Constable Cho enquired politely. He had his notebook poised to take on the spot comments.

'Well,' Doctor Macarthur said, 'it's obvious. Death was caused by the carotid artery being severed by a single blow to the neck from a sharp instrument, possibly a knife or a small hatchet.' He turned his head and regarded Mr Tan's neck from a different angle, 'No, probably not a hatchet. Perhaps a butcher's cleaver.' Constable Cho wrote down *'butcher's cleaver'*. 'No, not a butcher's cleaver, wrong configuration.' Cho crossed out *'butcher's cleaver'*. 'Have you ever seen a wound from a cleaver?'

Constable Cho nodded.

'More than one?'

Constable Cho nodded.

'Not a butcher's cleaver, is it?'

Constable Cho kept silent. It was not for him to offer suggestions.

'Not allowed to put ideas into my head, aye?' Macarthur said. 'Quite right. It's—' he knelt down and moved back a flap of skin from Tan's gaping throat (Constable Cho looked away. Tommy Lai put his handkerchief to his mouth and went into the back room), 'It's a—' he looked at Cho, 'it's a funny wound, isn't it?'

'Funny,' Constable Cho said. He was beginning to feel a little sick too. He wished Macarthur would hurry up so the photographers and fingerprint men from Scientific could come down, the ambulance could come down—in fact anyone could come down and he could go out.

'Very odd,' Doctor Macarthur said. 'It's a—' He moved the head that was only connected by courtesy to the dead neck, 'It's a—'

'It's a kukri,' Cho said. He had interviewed the assistant and the assistant knew what it had been, 'It's an Indian Gurkha kukri.'

'Quite right,' Macarthur said. 'Quite right.' He said, 'You

took the words out of my mouth.' He gazed at the wound for a final, fascinated time, 'Kukri, quite right. Of course it is.'

Constable Cho wrote down *Kukri* where, above it as part of Tommy Lai's statement, he had written down *Kukri*.

Down the road, behind a tram and an empty hearse, the gangsters' cars came. They drove very slowly and correctly and Feiffer, from his concealment in front of a parked Thunderbird car of dubious suspension, thought that was one charge he couldn't get them on. He shot a quick checking look across the road to where O'Yee crouched in front of a Volkswagen truck with Spencer and looked for Auden.

Auden lounged against the wall of the police station looking like a cop lounging against the wall of a police station pretending he was just lounging.

Feiffer glanced back down the street. A few people turned their heads to wonder what a European in a stained white suit was doing hiding in front of a Thunderbird car in Yellowthread Street. Constable Lee, on patrol behind the group of passing people, stopped.

He said, 'Sir?' but Feiffer reached over and pulled him down beside him. The group of people did not wonder what a European in a stained white suit was doing wrenching a uniformed Chinese policeman down beside him in front of a Thunderbird car in Yellowthread Street or why they watched three black cars cruise very legally and carefully towards them, they *knew*. They took to their heels and ran.

The first black car stopped. The second black car stopped. The third black car stopped.

'Stop them!' Feiffer ordered Lee, and Lee stepped out into the middle of the road, raised his hand, and said, 'Halt!'

The three black cars were already halted, so they did the next best thing: they roared into reverse.

Auden stopped lounging. He pushed himself off the wall and drew his revolver in the same moment, ran across the road, smashed the ribbed barrel of the heavy weapon through the side window of the first vehicle and said, 'Freeze!'

O'Yee at the open window of the second said, 'Don't move!' The third car made it into reverse. Feiffer drew his weapon and took aim at the front tyres. Spencer ran across his line of vision. He yelled, 'Spencer! Get out of the—' but Spencer continued to run directly between the car and Feiffer's line of fire. Constable Lee drew his own revolver and took a steady two handed aim at the driver of the reversing car.

He shouted at the top of his lungs in Chinese, 'Stop or die!' and then Spencer ran into his line of fire too. The third car swerved across the road, manoeuvring to turn and Ah Pin, behind Feiffer, shouted at him, 'My cousin! Don't shoot my cousin!'

Spencer had his own gun out. He waved it in the approximate direction of the driver. Spencer thought, 'A crime, I'm going to solve a crime,' and flung the pistol through the front windscreen. It landed on the seat on top of The Fourth Gangster in an explosion of breaking glass and fractured his kneecap.

The third driver, to wit, The Fourth Gangster, to wit, Ah Pin's cousin, to wit, Spencer's victim, grasped at his knee, slapped the gearstick into first, rammed at the accelerator with his broken knee joint and ran down a vegetable cart whose owner had fled and left it in the middle of the road, and in a cascade of melons, pears, and cabbages, The Fourth Gangster's car came to a halt as Constable Lee and Detective Inspector Spencer of the Thrown Revolver piled in to subdue him.

Feiffer holstered his gun and strolled over to the first car, against whose bonnet Mr Boon from Hanford Hill, Hernando Haw from Macao, and the Buddha figure of Low Fat stood with their legs and arms spreadeagled.

'Good morning,' Feiffer said to Mr Boon. 'Bit late for a drive, isn't it?'

Auden finished frisking Low Fat. He said to Feiffer, 'Nothing,' and did not object when Mr Boon released himself from his spreadeagled position and turned to face Feiffer.

'What did you say, sir?' Mr Boon enquired politely.

'Where are the guns?'

'Guns?' Mr Boon asked. It seemed the word was an unfamiliar one, 'Guns?'

'Guns,' Feiffer said, 'knives, bombs, cleavers, hatchets; you know: that sort of thing.' He glanced at O'Yee at the second car. O'Yee had The Club (With Nails), Shotgun Sen, Crushed Toes and Osaka Onuki against it, but it seemed they too wore nothing more lethal than their braces under their coats. O'Yee shook his head.

'I don't know what you mean,' Mr Boon said, 'but we'll pay the ransom anyway.'

'What ransom?'

'The ransom respectable businessmen pay when Hong Kong gangsters kidnap them,' Hernando Haw said. He straightened up and turned around, 'We only ask to be returned to the bosoms of our wives and children. Nothing more.'

'You people are the gangsters.'

'Us?' Mr Boon asked incredulously, 'Us?' He turned to Low Fat, 'Did you hear what this dishevelled person said?'

'No,' Low Fat said. He got up from his lean against the car, 'What did he say?'

'He said we were gangsters.'

Low Fat's face registered a total inability to credit the information. 'Then who are these people if we are the gangsters?' he asked in a tone of bewilderment.

Feiffer drew a breath. 'We are the fucking police!'

'I haven't been doing any fucking,' Low Fat said, 'I've been taking a drive.'

Feiffer glanced back at O'Yee. O'Yee shook his head for the second time.

'May we be on our way?' Mr Boon asked.

'No,' Feiffer said. He looked desperately towards the third car. Shadows moved behind the shattered windscreen, but no one came out.

'I want to search your car,' Feiffer said.

Mr Boon sighed. 'If you wish.' He stood to one side of the door to allow Feiffer admission. He looked at his watch, 'Please do not detain us too long with this routine checking of traffic that passes down Yellowthread Street in order to gather information for the placement of Stop signs and pedestrian crossings.' He smiled evilly.

Feiffer glanced back at the third car. He saw Spencer come out. Spencer held up something in his hand and said, 'Inspector Feiffer!' It was, Feiffer was delighted to behold, a wooden club (with nails).

Feiffer smiled evilly at Mr Boon. 'Well, well, well,' he said, 'a club.'

'With nails in it,' Hernando Haw added. He had keener eyes than the rest.

'You don't say so!' Mr Boon said. 'My goodness, the streets aren't safe.'

Spencer held up his second trophy.

'And a sawed off shotgun,' Feiffer said.

Constable Lee held up The Fourth Gangster and supported him across the road.

'And one gangster,' Feiffer said. Someone's eighty-year-old voice cried, 'Cousin!'

'With relatives,' Mr Boon said. 'Really, this is all absolutely fascinating.' He turned to Low Fat and patted him on the shoulder, 'This is *life*, my friend. What an education for us boring commercial people: life in the raw.'

'Hmm,' Low Fat said. He wondered if he had done the right thing about Tinkerbell Lin Wong. Anyone who could satisfy a Mongolian who went around chopping off ears, fingers and heads— 'Well,' he thought, 'maybe I made a mistake there ...'

Spencer held up three pistols: two Mausers and a Luger. He dropped the Luger on to the road. It didn't go off. He picked it up, returned the handguns to the seat of the car, and displayed a sword and a hatchet. 'My goodness!' Mr Boon said, 'It's an arsenal that man in the third black car that coincidentally looks like ours whom we do not know and have never seen before has. Is it not, Mr Haw?'

'An arsenal,' Mr Haw said. 'That man who you have just arrested does not know us and we do not know him. He will not say he knows us.'

'Won't he?' Feiffer asked.

'He will not,' Mr Boon said.

'Oh? Why is that?'

'Because he does not know us,' Low Fat said. He checked with Mr Boon: 'How was that?'

'Admirable,' Mr Boon said. 'Perfectly expressed.'

'Where are the other two cars?'

'Indeed,' Mr Boon said.

'Yes,' Hernando Haw agreed.

'What other two cars?' Low Fat asked.

'Indeed,' Mr Boon said.

Hernando Haw said, 'Yes. What other two cars?'

Mr Boon said, 'Indeed.'

Feiffer looked at Mr Boon. He knew when he was beaten. He said lamely, 'You keep your people away from Camphorwood Lane or there'll be trouble for you.'

'A good citizen obeys the instructions of the police,' Mr Boon said. (Feiffer thought, 'I'm not starting that again.') 'We will, of course, take your advice,' Mr Boon said.

'We will get back into our vehicles now and proceed on our peaceful way,' Hernando Haw said. He smiled. Mr Boon gave him a warning look: enough was enough. 'Yes, sir,' Hernando Haw said to Inspector Feiffer. He got into the car.

Feiffer held Mr Boon's eyes. Feiffer said, 'Don't put in a claim for compensation for the broken window, Boon.'

Mr Boon raised his hands to Heaven. A broken window was the least an honest citizen could donate to the cause of capturing a dangerous gun-runner loose in the streets.

'O.K.,' Feiffer said, 'You and your friends piss off.' He watched as the two cars went down the street.

O'Yee came over to join him. He said, 'At least we got their weapons.' He said, 'That's something.'

It may have been, but it wasn't much. The two carloads of gangsters drove unerringly to a fish stall minus their guns, knives, hatchets, clubs (with nails), and their Japanese short sword and picked up from the owner of the stall guns, knives, hatchets, a club (with nails), and—the stall owner didn't even blink at the request—a Japanese short sword.

Then they rendezvoused with the other two black cars in Canton Street and continued on their original journey to Camphorwood Lane to kill the Mongolian.

The first thing Mrs Skilbeck saw as she passed the parked Thunderbird in front of the Police Station was the two dumb cops standing out in the middle of the road looking at a mess of squashed melons, mashed cabbages, and run-over pears.

She said in a very loud voice that carried above the traffic, *'Hey, you cops!'*

Feiffer turned around. He saw Mrs Skilbeck.

'You're standing in the middle of the road, you dumb cops!' Mrs Skilbeck yelled.

The dumb cops walked back to the footpath.

'You guys,' Mrs Skilbeck said with undisguised dissatisfaction, 'You guys are nuts! Do you know that?'

'We know,' O'Yee said.

'It's three o'clock in the morning,' Mrs Skilbeck said. 'Doesn't that mean anything to you people?' She paused on the steps of the police station. A telephone inside rang insistently.

'Someone keeps telephoning me,' Feiffer said. He was thinking about the gangsters. He said, 'I keep hanging up.'

Mrs Skilbeck looked at him. She did not pause, she stopped. She said with feeling, 'You people are nuts. The only one of you people who isn't nuts is that little Chinese girl.' She stormed into the Police Station where Minnie Oh held an enormous Webley .455 revolver trained on the front door. She held it up with two hands and aimed it at the middle of Mrs Skilbeck's forehead.

She said fiercely, 'I'm ready. Let them come.'

Mrs Skilbeck went limp.

'It's all over,' Feiffer said. He deposited Mrs Skilbeck in a chair. Minnie Oh put down the giant revolver with relief and rubbed painfully at her wrist tendons. She said, 'It was the only one I could find. No one told me—'

'O.K.,' Feiffer said. He said, 'You better get a cup of tea or something for the lady,' and went over to hang up his ringing telephone.

He got Spencer and Auden up from the cells where they were giving first aid to The Fourth Gangster and sent them around to Camphorwood Lane on foot.

The Mongolian saw the gangsters come. They came in two black cars and stopped at the western end of Camphorwood Lane. The Mongolian glanced over the parapet of the flat roof on which he lived to the other end of Camphorwood Lane. Two more black cars came and stopped at the eastern end. No one got out. They sat in their cars and orders were given and arranged.

The Mongolian was not sure who they were. Some of the goldsmiths came out of their shops alerted by telephone calls between themselves and they looked at the black cars and smiled. Then they went back inside their shops and drew the blinds and the *CLOSED* signs on their glass doors. They walked past the four black cars, two at either end of the street, and went away. The street went quiet.

Behind the Mongolian, on the roof, half a dozen families slept fitfully on blankets and padded Chinese quilts. A game of Mah-Jong was in progress in the far corner of the area and the white bone tiles went slap! slap! slap! as the players smashed them down zestfully on to a plywood table.

One of the men from the black cars got out and looked up at the roof. He looked back into the front seat of the car and nodded in response to an order. Then someone else in the back of the car handed him an object that he put under his coat. The object was long and black and it went under the coat snugly. The Mongolian pursed his lips and smiled a faint smile. The man with the black object under his coat came probingly across the street and disappeared into a building next door to the Mongolian's building. The Mongolian pursed his lips and shook his head in amusement. He went unhurriedly across to the other side of the roof and waited for the man to appear.

'You people are nuts,' Mrs Skilbeck said weakly. She put the teacup down on a chair next to hers with disgust. 'And I don't like British tea.'

'It's Chinese tea,' Constable Lee said. He smiled ingratiatingly at Minnie, 'Constable Oh made it for you herself.'

Mrs Skilbeck looked at Constable Oh. She was another nut. Mrs Skilbeck said, 'No wonder you people can't find anything.' She said, 'I've had nothing but humiliating experiences ever since I got to this goddamned place.'

'We're very sorry,' Minnie Oh said sweetly.

'So am I!' Mrs Skilbeck said suddenly loudly. Inexplicably, there were tears glistening in her eyes. 'Where the hell's my husband?'

'We've had other things on our minds,' O'Yee said. He thought if Spencer and Auden—*Bill* and *Phil*—weren't here it behoved someone to defend poor Minnie. 'We've been a little busy arresting criminals.' He flipped through the papers in the Pending tray absently and read one. He said without changing his tone, 'Your husband comes up before the Magistrate in the morning.'

'What?' Mrs Skilbeck said.

Minnie Oh said, 'What?'

Constable Lee said—

'In the morning,' O'Yee said. 'Charged with being drunk and disorderly in a common brothel, attempted rape, assaulting a police officer, and resisting arrest.'

'What?' Mrs Skilbeck said.

'In the morning,' O'Yee said. The telephone rang and he turned around to pick it up. He said to Feiffer, 'It's for you.' He said, 'Herman A. Skilbeck, New Jersey, United States of America.' He said, 'My parents live in San Francisco.' He said, 'We probably won't proceed with the rape charge.'

'The rape charge ...' Mrs Skilbeck echoed.

'We won't proceed,' O'Yee said. Feiffer said, 'Feiffer,' into the phone. He hoped it might be Nicola suffering from insomnia.

'You can see him in the morning,' O'Yee said. 'We won't oppose a reasonable bail provided he hands in his passport and onward tickets.'

'Feiffer,' Feiffer said into the phone for a second time, 'Hullo?'

'Oh,' Mrs Skilbeck said. She picked up the teacup and drank the contents without remembering that Chinese tea disgusted her. 'Oh,' Mrs Skilbeck said.

'Feiffer,' Feiffer said for the third time, 'Is there anyone there?'

'Ha!' the voice on the other end of the line said in triumph and slammed the receiver down.

'Oh,' Mrs Skilbeck said. She got unsteadily to her feet and said uncharacteristically quietly, 'Oh.' She gazed at the Police Station interior. She said very softly, 'Oh.' She said to Minnie Oh, 'I think I'll go home now.'

'Can we drive you?' Constable Lee asked sympathetically. Mrs Skilbeck patted him on the shoulder and said, 'No, thank you, dear,' then patted him again. She went carefully across the room and down the steps to the sidewalk.

'We didn't get her address!' Constable Lee said. He began to go after her.

Minnie raised her hand to stop him. She understood women. She said, 'She'll be back in the morning,' and then she patted Constable Lee on the shoulder too.

Constable Lee thought he had done something. He wasn't sure what it was. He wished he knew how to do it again.

The roof next to the flat roof was pitched and uninhabited. The gangster came out there and checked the loads in his sawed off shotgun. He glanced across at the Mah-Jong players and the sleepers, but he didn't see the Mongolian.

Someone tapped him gently on the shoulder. Shotgun Sen said without turning around, 'I can't see him. Got any ideas?' He thought, 'Wait a minute, I came up alone—!'

First the Mah-Jong players came out of the building and ran away down the street, then something was thrown over the parapet of the flat roof and landed in the middle of the road near the cars at the western end of Camphorwood Lane, then Hernando Haw identified the something as what was left of Shotgun Sen, then Low Fat said, 'Bad—' then the Mongolian opened fire on the two cars with Sen's sawed off shotgun, then the sleepers and the residents woke and came running out of the building.

The Mongolian stood in full silhouette on the flat roof pumping lead into the street and reloading from Shotgun Sen's captured belt of cartridges.

Then Constable Cho ran out into the street, collected a charge of twelve-gauge pellets full in the chest and fell over.

Mr Boon scrabbled out of his car and took cover on the protected side of the insubstantial metal from one of Mr Ford's Asian factories and shouted to his colleagues at both ends of the street, 'Kill him!'

The Medical Examiner ran out of *Edgar Tan and Company* to give assistance to Constable Cho. A blast of pellets whizzed past him and he stopped. The Mongolian levelled the weapon at him again for a second shot and pressed the trigger. The gun went *click*! The Mongolian reached for another two cartridges. The belt was empty. Doctor Macarthur looked at him. The Mongolian screamed something and threw the shotgun. It landed on the ground next to the Doctor and snapped across the breach. Doctor Macarthur went to Constable Cho. Constable Cho was dead. A singularly nasty-looking Oriental person went past Doctor Macarthur firing an enormous pistol with a shoulder stock at someone and then another person ran by wielding a lignum vitae club with nails sticking out of it and Doctor Macarthur threw himself flat on the ground and stayed there.

The last of the residents came running out of the building holding screaming children and disappeared around the Lane into Canton Street on their way out of the Second World War. A Japanese shrieking something in Japanese rushed into the building across the street carrying a short sword. Doctor Macarthur heard his war cry inside the building, then the Japanese staggered back out of the building without his sword, holding his arm in his right hand. Doctor Macarthur put his hands over his head and kissed and hugged the roadway. Then something clicked inside his anatomically-qualified mind and he stole a quick second glance at the Japanese arm. The Japanese had dropped it. It lay on the ground still wearing a wristwatch.

The Japanese shrieked something else in Japanese and lay down next to his arm and died. There were four shots inside the building, then about forty, then another scream, then more shots.

Mr Boon said to Mr Haw, 'He almost shot me.'

Mr Haw leaned over from his ground-loving position on the sidewalk and said, 'Yeah.' He said, highly offended, 'Me too.'

'He almost shot me,' Mr Boon said again.

'He's killed Onuki and Sen and the cop,' Mr Haw said. He said to Low Fat on the ground next to him, 'Did he kill the cop?'

'He killed the cop,' Low Fat said.

'He almost shot me,' Mr Boon said. Nothing like this had ever happened to him before and he was very shocked. He said, 'He almost shot me, Hernando.'

Across the street, the building now housed six very active gangsters and an even more active Mongolian and there was the sound of much running on its old staircases, much shouting reverberated inside its yellowed wooden walls, and there were more gunshots.

'Very bad,' Low Fat said. He said, 'Not good.'

'Bad about the cop,' Hernando Haw said. He said, 'We're on the side of law and order now.'

Mr Boon only replied, 'He almost shot me.' He put his hand across his eyes in shame and mortification.

The shooting and shouting continued.

Down at the single water tap near the resettlement area in Hop Pei Cove, the first of the trouble started. The first squad of Riot Police put out their cigarettes, donned their helmets, and went in to quell it.

Feiffer's phone rang. He picked it up and said, 'Feiffer.'

'Ah!' the drunken voice said again, 'Ah! It's me.'

'Who is "me"?'

'Ha!' the voice said. It sounded like it was going to be a very basic conversation.

'Listen, "Ha!" I'm getting more than a little tired of maniacs ringing me up just to say "Ha!"'

'Ha!' the voice said, 'Ha! Ha!' The voice said, 'I'm going to get you, Feiffer.'

'Good for you,' Feiffer said. He listened for background noises the way blindfolded kidnap victims did in the movies and on television, but there weren't any background noises: no level crossing bells, no tug boat engines, no sovereigns or pieces of eight clinking away in a nearby gold market, no steam compressor hisses—in fact, none of the things movie and television cops found it impossible to trace phone calls and kidnap victims without. There was only a drunken voice saying, 'Ha!' at past three o'clock in the morning.

'Are there any steam compressors or level crossing bells or tug boats around there?' Feiffer asked cordially. He thought O'Yee would be better at this than him. He was the movie buff with the free ticket to a twelve-month sentence of matinees at the Peacock Cinema.

'What?' the drunken voice said, 'Any what?' He said, 'Don't try to trace this call!'

'I wasn't going to.'

'It won't work!'

Feiffer thought of the response he would get from the Post Office if he tried to get half a dozen of their engineers out of bed in the middle of the night to trace a drunk saying, 'Ha!' in a public telephone box. He said, 'It never does.'

'That's sensible of you.'

'I'm glad you think so.' He said, 'Do you happen to speak English?'

'Of course I do!'

'O.K.,' Feiffer said in English, 'Who was the first Tudor king of England?'

'What?'

'I said, if you speak English, what was the name of the first Tudor king of England?'

'I'm an educated man!' the drunken voice said, 'I wasn't always a—' He said, 'I'm an educated man!'

'O.K.,' Feiffer said, 'I repeat, what was the name of the first Tudor king of England?'

'I learnt all this at school. I went to an English school here before my family fell on—'

'I can tell,' Feiffer said. 'The name of the first Tudor king of England.'

'Henry the Fourth!'

'The second?'

'Henry the Fifth!'

'The third?'

'Henry the Sixth!'

'Wonderful!' Feiffer said. 'Just the names will do. The Stuarts.'

'The Stuarts?'

'Yes. The name of the first Stuart king.'

'James!'

'The name of the second?'

'Charles!'

'The name of the third?'

'Charles again!'

'The name of the fourth?'

'James!'

'Your name?'

'Lop!'

—there was a pause.

'Thank you,' Feiffer said. 'How is everything in Cat Street these days?'

'You put the tax man on to me,' Lop said. His voice was quieter. He said, 'You put the tax man on to me...'

'Wrong,' Feiffer said. He said, 'I've enjoyed our little chats. Goodnight.'

And he hung up.

The phone rang again.

'Listen!' Feiffer roared into the phone, 'Do you want to be charged?'

'Yes, please,' Nicola said, 'and I'd like to serve my sentence in bed with you if that's all right.'

'Yeah,' Feiffer said. He let out a breath and calmed. 'That's just fine. What would you like to be charged with?'

'How about simmering sexuality?'

'You already are,' Feiffer said.

'Then why don't you come home to a little of it?'

'Can't you sleep?'

'Is that the best response you can manage?'

Feiffer smiled.

'Are you smiling?'

'Yes.'

The phone on O'Yee's desk rang. He said, 'Yellowthread Pol—' He held the instrument up to Feiffer. He said, 'Guess who?'

'It isn't Nicola,' Feiffer said, and Nicola said, 'Then who

the bloody hell do you think it is?' Feiffer said, 'The other phone.' He said, 'Can you hold on a bit?'

'No,' Nicola said. She hung up. Feiffer said, 'Shit!' and picked up the other phone. He said into it, 'This had better be of bloody earth-shattering importance or I'll stick it up your—'

'Good evening, Inspector Feiffer,' Sister Sung's voice said, 'this is Sister Sung from St Paul de Chartres Hospital and you should be ashamed.'

'I am,' Feiffer said, 'I was having a very randy telephone conversation with my wife.'

'How is Nicola?'

'Simmering with sexuality.'

Sister Sung said, 'Are you trying to embarrass me, Inspector?'

'Yes,' Feiffer said, 'I apologise.'

'I wasn't always a nun, you know.'

'I know. I wasn't always rude to people. I'm sorry, Sister. How can I help you?'

Sister Sung said, 'I can well imagine Nicola simmering with sexuality. She's a very healthy girl.'

'Hmm,' Feiffer said.

Sister Sung said, 'You know of course that Alice Ping discharged herself?'

'I didn't, as a matter of fact.'

'You weren't told?'

'There wasn't any reason. She was the victim, wasn't she? This time. So far as I know at the moment she's officially as pure as the driven snow.'

'Quite,' Sister Sung said, 'The only thing is, she discharged herself without telling us and one of our wheelchairs is missing.'

'Alice pinched a wheelchair?'

'Well, I wouldn't exactly put it that way,' Sister Sung said with the full weight of her Christian understanding. 'Let us say that she was given a wheelchair in which to rest and she may have decided that she could rest better at home. I wonder if you could ask her to bring it back? They're in rather short supply.'

'I will,' Feiffer said.

'Give my regards to Nicola.'

'I will,' Feiffer said. He thought it best not to add anything.

Sister Sung waited for him to add something. He resisted the temptation. She said, 'Thank you, Inspector, and good-night. I'll pray for you.'

'Thanks,' Feiffer said and his own phone rang again.

Feiffer's voice felt like an old tennis shoe that had lost its bounce. He said, 'This is the Lone Ranger, who's that?'

'I'm going to get you anyway!'

'Oh, Christ, not you again!' He hung up and the phone immediately rang again.

When Auden and Spencer arrived in Camphorwood Lane the first thing they saw was a gaggle of middle-aged gangsters on the sidewalk holding on to their ears. They thought it was a funny sight. Then they saw Cho dead on the road and they did not think that was funny at all. A fusillade of gunshots echoed inside the old building across the road and on the road there was a Government Medical Examiner with a Roman nose taking cover half a dozen yards from the detached arm of a dead Japanese assassin. Auden drew his Colt Python and took cover behind the shotgun-riddled second car of the gangsters. A second eruption of gunshots came from inside the building and he began running down the street past the crouching middle-aged gangsters towards a telephone. The only shop still open was *Edgar Tan and Company* and he kicked the half-open glass door off its hinges and reached for the telephone on the counter. He glanced across and couldn't see Spencer. He began dialling the number of Yellowthread Street.

Feiffer picked up the ringing telephone. He said, 'Yes?'

'Riot Squard,' a voice said. 'Who is this?'

'This is Detective Chief Inspector Feiffer,' Feiffer said. He thought, 'People keep ringing me up.'

'Riot Squad,' the voice said again. Maybe he liked the sound of it. 'This is Constable Yan of the Riot Squad'—he did like the sound of it—'I have a message from Superintendent Algy.'

'O.K.,' Feiffer said, 'then let's have it.'

Constable Yan took a deep breath at the other end of the phone. Feiffer thought he was thinking of a way to get 'Riot Squad' into his conversation again. Constable Yan said, 'The Riot Squad have taken up positions at the water tap near the Hong Bay resettlement area—'

'I already know that.'

'—and this is to inform you that at present elements of the—'

'Riot Squad,' Feiffer said helpfully.

'Yes. Elements of the Riot Squad are at present dealing with a disturbance in that area.' He paused. 'That's the message.'

'Sir,' Feiffer prompted.

'Pardon?'

'Sir. You say, "Sir", to an Inspector, even if he is only a member of the ordinary, non-Riot Squad variety. Don't they teach you that at Fanling?'

'Yes, sir,' Constable Yan snapped. 'Sorry, sir. Yes, sir, they do teach that.'

Feiffer thought, 'I sound like Captain Queeg.' He said, 'I used to be a member of the Squad myself at one time.'

'Really, sir?' Yan was impressed.

'I'll send some men down right away,' Feiffer said. 'Pass that on to Superintendent Algy, would you?'

'No—!' Constable Yan said. He sounded shocked at the suggestion. 'We don't need any assistance—' ('So much for the "Sir",' Feiffer thought) 'We have the matter entirely under control.'

'Then why tell me about it?'

That fazed him. Constable Yan couldn't think of a reason in the world why a permanent member of the Riot Squad would want to tell a member of the ordinary, foot-slogging variety of unchosen policeman anything. He said, 'I really couldn't say.'

'You don't know?'

'No.'

'I'll tell Superintendent Algy that,' Feiffer said and hung up as the telephone on O'Yee's desk rang again and O'Yee handed it over wordlessly.

'I'm just around the corner—' Lop's voice said.

'Oh, Jesus Christ!'

'—and I'm coming to get you!'

'You're driving me bloody mad!'

The telephone on Feiffer's desk rang. Feiffer took O'Yee by the scruff of the neck and propelled him to it. 'You!' Feiffer said to O'Yee.

'Am I?' Lop asked.

'Are you what?'

'Driving you mad?'

'Yes!'

'Good,' Lop said. 'Then I'm temporarily satisfied. Goodnight.' And he hung up.

O'Yee said, 'Inspector O'—' then listened.

'If I ever get my hands on that Cat Street bar-owning bastard Lop I'm going to murder him!' Feiffer said to O'Yee.

O'Yee wasn't listening. He held the receiver away from his ear and said, 'Cho's dead. They're in Camphorwood Lane with guns.' He said, 'People have been killed.'

Through the instrument, five feet away, Feiffer could actually hear the shots.

The Mongolian was still in the building. He was on the fourth floor. The gangsters were still in the building. They were on the ground, first, second and third floors. Coming up. The Mongolian craned his head over the rickety wooden balustrade on the fourth floor and saw the gangsters form a knot at the beginning of the corridor on the third floor. They had a hurried conference and then went to kick all the doors down.

He heard the doors go smash! smash! smash! one after another then there were three simultaneous bursts of gunfire and then nothing. He saw the gangsters go back to the start of the corridor (saw their shadows reflected on the wall in the light of the single naked bulb on each floor). The gangsters had another conference then went back down the corridor. They must have found another door. It went smash! as they kicked it in. There was no gunfire. It must have been a closet or a toilet. The closet or toilet door went smash! again as one of the gangsters kicked it a second time for good measure.

The Mongolian started laughing: harsh, rasping cackles. The gangsters made a series of surprised noises to each other and looked up at the fourth floor. The Mongolian ducked his head back and went into the third room on the fourth floor and left the door ajar a quarter of an inch. Then he opened the far window in the mattress-crowded room, turned the light off, and stood to one side of the door.

He waited.

Auden saw Spencer. Spencer was against the wall of the building, moving towards the door with his gun out. Auden yelled, 'Spencer!'

Spencer looked over.

Auden yelled, 'Get back here!'

Spencer hesitated. He glanced towards the open door to the building and then down to his cocked service revolver. He glanced back along the street to the pellet-holed cars and then he looked again at Auden.

'Get back here!' Auden yelled. He had cover in the doorway of *Edgar Tan and Company*. He yelled, 'Bloody well get back here!'

Spencer ducked his head and started to run across the road. He glanced at Cho's body as he went past. Cho was dead. He glanced at Doctor Macarthur's body as he went past.

Doctor Macarthur was alive. Spencer said, 'Come on, Doctor!'

'Like hell I will!'

Spencer stopped. He reached down and took Macarthur by the arm. He said encouragingly, 'I'll look after you—come on now—'

'Like hell you will!' Macarthur said and didn't move.

From inside the building across the road there was a burst of gunfire as one of the gangsters sprayed the stairway to the fourth floor with automatic fire. He had an old Thompson sub-machine gun. The bullets went chop! chop! chop! into the rotting staircase and tore strips of splintered wood off it.

'Get into cover!' Spencer said. 'They'll kill you here!'

'Like hell they will!' Macarthur said and got to his feet. He ran across the road into cover.

'Hell!' Spencer said, and ran after him.

The doctor made it to the doorway of *Edgar Tan's*. Auden said, 'Doctor—' but the doctor did not stop. He continued directly into the store and threw himself down alongside what was left of Edgar Tan. The floor of the room was like a post-mortem table after a post-mortem. He felt at home.

'What did you think you were doing?' Auden demanded. He pulled Spencer into the doorway and waved irritably at him to holster his cocked revolver.

Spencer said —

'You're a cop, not a bloody member of the bloody KGB!' He said, 'Are you out of your bloody mind?'

Spencer said —

There was another heavy, slow burst from the Thompson.

'What the hell did you think you were doing?'

Spencer said —

Auden looked quickly down the road.

Auden said, 'We're not going in there until reinforcements arrive. What the blazes did you think you were playing at?'

Spencer did not reply.

Auden said, 'What we're going to do is go down and find out from Mr Boon and his friends just what the hell's happening in there. No private heroics, all right?'

Spencer said —

'Down the road,' Auden said, and push-started Spencer in the right direction.

'I just thought—' Spencer said.

Auden said, 'Shut up, stupid!'

The gangsters—there were six of them including Crushed Toes, The Club (With Nails) and the four who had come from the cars at the eastern end of the street—stopped in front of the first door on the fourth floor.

The Mongolian heard them. They were two doors away. He cackled quietly to himself.

'O.K.,' The Club (With Nails) said. The man with the Thompson took aim at the centre of the door. The others moved aside to give him room. The man with the Thompson was called The Chopper Man.

Auden reached the quivering, laid-side-by-side figures of Mr Boon and his two friends. He grabbed the first of them, who happened to be Low Fat, under the arms and dragged him to his feet. Low Fat's legs were jelly. Auden propped him up against the side of the car.

'How many?' Auden said. He held up Low Fat with his outstretched arm.

'Aye?' Low Fat said. His ears were poor. All those gunshots.

'Your people,' Auden said. He said again, 'How many?'

'Aye?' Low Fat said. 'Not my people.'

'Whose people?' He indicated Hernando Haw with a jerking movement of his head. He said to Spencer, 'Pick him up!'

Spencer picked him up. He went into position alongside Low Fat on the car like the second in a row of encoffined murderers in Madame Tussaud's waxworks.

Auden said, 'How many?' and hit Low Fat.

Auden said to Hernando Haw, 'How many?'

Hernando Haw looked at the hit Low Fat.

Auden said to Spencer, 'Hit him.'

'Six!' Hernando Haw said. 'Six!'

'Not our people,' Mr Boon said from the sidewalk. Auden went over to pick him up. Low Fat fell down.

'Not our people,' Hernando Haw said.

Auden said to Spencer, 'Hit him!'

Spencer hesitated. He said, 'I couldn't do that, Phil—'

'Who killed the cop?' Auden said to Mr Boon. He dragged Mr Boon to his feet. He said, 'Which one of you bastards killed the cop?'

Spencer said, 'I just can't bring myself to hit someone who's—'

'The Mongolian,' Mr Boon said. He was afraid of being hit, 'The Mongolian killed him. We're on the side of law and order—'

'You're innocent?'

'We are,' Mr Boon said. 'There isn't a reason in the world why you should hit any of us—'

'Right,' Auden said. He hit Mr Boon.

The Chopper Man kicked the door down and chopped the room to pieces with the Thompson gun. The room fell to bits and spewed out smoke and dust. A flurry of empty cartridge-cases flew out from the ejection port of the big gun, tinkled on to the floor, and rolled away over the edge of the corridor, a fortune in brass gone down three flights of nothingness to the ground floor, and scattered to the four winds and the rats.

The smoke cleared and the six gangsters glanced in.

'Empty,' Crushed Toes pronounced. He jerked his thumb in the direction of the next room, 'Next.'

The Chopper Man fitted another magazine of rimless .45 calibre cartridges into his chopper. He hauled back on the cocking lever.

Auden pulled his Colt Python on the three gang bosses and snapped, 'Don't move.'

Low Fat was still doubled up in pain on the sidewalk and he didn't move. Mr Boon was doubled up in pain against the side of the car and he didn't move. Hernando Haw looked down into the yawning cavern of the Colt's .357 magnum barrel and he didn't move. Spencer released his hold on him. Hernando Haw had a clearer picture of the entire gun. He moved. He doubled up in pain against the car and didn't move.

Spencer looked interrogatively at Auden. The gun wasn't pointing at him so he didn't notice it. He said to Auden, 'I didn't even touch him—' He asked, 'Did I?'

Auden cocked the hammer of his Colt and thought of the squat magnum round lying directly after the regulation .38.

He said to Spencer, 'Shut up.'

There was a tiny hole in the wall of the Mongolian's hiding place. He could see into the second room. It was in darkness. He heard the gangsters stop outside the second room and he chuckled.

'O.K.,' Crushed Toes said to The Chopper Man outside the second room.

The door smashed open and the room lit up. The bullets went chop! chop! chop! choppety-chop! chop! chop! chop! into the walls of the room. The Chopper Man was lit up in his own muzzle flashes. He looked like a madman working a blast furnace. The Mongolian moved his stomach up and down with mirth. He did a little dance with his eye still to the wall. He said, 'Eeee-eee-ee!' to himself and juggled his belly up and down in merriment. The flashes stopped. The ejected brass cases went tinkle, tinkle, on to the floor outside the room and a shadow peered into the darkened room and said, 'Empty.'

The shadow went away. The Mongolian hammered his fists silently on the wall and did a little dance. He went over to his old position to one side of the door and rubbed his fingers against his palms in anticipation.

A voice outside said, 'Next,' and the Mongolian moved towards the door.

The Chopper Man inserted a fresh magazine into his chopper and drew back the cocking handle. The gangsters stood poised outside the door to the third room.

The Mongolian moved forward to the door and laid his hand gently on the knob.

Crushed Toes stood to one side of the third door and drew a breath. There was only one more floor to go after this. He nodded his head to The Chopper Man and said, 'O.K.' and the Mongolian came out of the room like an express train.

The Mongolian shrieked, 'Aaahhh!' and hammered one of the gangsters in the throat with his fist. The gangster went into the wooden railing and smashed it. It shattered into kindling and sailed off into the abyss of the stairwell drop down four floors. The gangster went after it. The Chopper Man said, 'Ut—!' and the Mongolian hammered him in the groin and sent him flying into the kicked-down door of the second room. The Club (With Nails) raised his club. The Mongolian wrenched it off him and threw it after The Chopper Man. The Chopper Man's chopper lay where The Chopper Man had dropped it: at the Mongolian's feet. One of the eastern-end parked car gangsters drew his pistol. The Mongolian reached down and drew the chopper. The eastern-end parked car gangster aimed his pistol. The Mongolian pressed the trigger of the chopper and turned him into a blur. The bolt went click on an empty magazine. The Mongolian threw the gun at Crushed Toes. It missed. Crushed Toes had his own gun out. It was a broom-handled Mauser automatic. He couldn't get the hammer back. The Mongolian hit him and knocked him against the remaining two gangsters. Crushed Toes got the hammer back in midflight and levelled it at the Mongolian, but the Mongolian stepped back inside the third room and slammed the door, and when the gangsters had put themselves together sufficiently to smash down the door he had gone out the open window to the fire escape, which way, up or down, they did not know.

The four remaining gangsters picked up themselves, their weapons, The Chopper Man and The Chopper Man's chopper, and huddled in mid-battle for a conference.

Feiffer saw Cho's body in the middle of the roadway. A stream of blood had coursed from it while Cho had been in the quick process of dying, but now that he was dead it had stopped. The Japanese, too, was dead. Just inside the doorway to *Edgar Tan and Company*, Edgar Tan was dead. Feiffer said to Mr Boon, and Mr Haw, and Low Fat, 'You three are under arrest just for a start.'

He and O'Yee had picked up Constable Sun from patrol on their way to Camphorwood Lane, so it was Feiffer, O'Yee, and two constables, Mr Boon and his friends faced, not to mention Auden and Spencer, and most certainly not to mention Auden's big gun.

Mr Boon said, 'Our lawyers will—'

'Shut up!' Feiffer said. He said to Auden, 'You hit them didn't you?'

'Yes!' Mr Boon said, 'he hit us!'

'Good,' Feiffer said. He ordered the two constables to put them into the paddy wagon they had come in. He said to Auden, 'Well?' He looked over at the temporarily silent building. 'They're in that building over there. Right?'

'Right.'

'How many?'

'Six.'

'Plus the Mongolian.'

Auden nodded. 'Plus the Mongolian. I think the Mongolian's done most of the killing.'

'Cho?'

'I think so. Either him or Sen. One of Boon's little helpers. They call him Shotgun Sen. That was what killed Cho.'

'Where's Sen now?'

Auden indicated a dark patch of something on the roadway. It looked like an old blanket someone had set fire to, stomped on, and then pulverised with rocks. Auden said, 'That's him there. More or less. The Mongolian again.'

Feiffer's eyes stayed on the body of Constable Cho. He asked O'Yee, 'Did you know him well?'

O'Yee shook his head.

'Neither did I. Married?'

O'Yee shrugged.

'He was,' Spencer said, 'I met his wife once in Nathan Road. He had two children.'

The two constables came back, Sun and Lee. They both looked at where Cho's body lay. Constable Sun said, 'We can get the body, Inspector.' They also knew he had a wife and two children, more familiarly than a chance meeting in Nathan Road. Constable Lee said, 'He was a friend of ours.'

Feiffer glanced at the building. 'First we get the people who did it.' He said to Lee and Sun, 'They're in that building.'

'They're armed,' Constable Lee stated as a rehearsal for the coroner's inquest which would ask why it was that he and Constable Sun had been unable to wound any of the people, only kill them. He drew his pistol. He said, 'Sun and I'll go in, Inspector.'

'We're going to do this properly,' Feiffer said. 'We're going to converge on the inside of the building in a logical way and we're going to arrest everyone inside, whoever they are.'

'If possible,' Constable Lee said. He looked to Inspector O'Yee for support.

O'Yee said, 'Policemen get killed the same as anyone else—'

Constable Sun said, 'Yes, sir.' He drew his pistol as well.

'O.K.,' Feiffer said. He considered the building and the other structures around it, 'O.K., this is the way we'll do it . . .'

He thought to himself, 'And I'd better be right.' He caught the look on Spencer's face: frightened. And Auden: anxious to try out that damned gun of his. And O'Yee: he had already had one gun, real or not, pointed at him so far tonight. And the two constables—

He thought, 'I'd better be right the first time,' and wondered what he himself looked like right about now.

'Yellowthread Street Police Station, WPC Oh speaking.'

'Minnie?' Nicola Feiffer's voice queried, 'this is Nicola Feiffer. Is my husband there?'

'No, Mrs Feiffer,' Minnie said. She was the only one there. 'He is out at the moment. Should you not be asleep? Is anything the matter?'

'No,' Nicola's voice said, 'I should be asleep. It's almost four o'clock in the morning.' She said, 'I suffer from insomnia when Inspector Feiffer's on night duty.' She said, 'You're not married, Minnie?'

'No.'

'Do you know where he's gone? Do you expect—'

'I could not say, Mrs Feiffer.' She glanced at the printed notices she had marked for distribution to the roof-top schools in the morning. Incongruously, they dealt with the need for road safety on the way to school. She said, 'It is only a routine matter, I think.'

'So are the multitudinous seas incarnadine.' She said, 'Do you know what an ounce is, Minnie?'

'It is a European measurement of weight.'

There was a brief silence on the line. Mrs Feiffer said, 'I'm sorry I—' She said, '—disturbed you. It was just that—'

'Everything is very quiet here, Mrs Feiffer,' Minnie lied. 'It is probably just a routine matter. Inspector Feiffer will be back soon I am certain.'

'Is Inspector O'Yee there to keep you running about for him?'

'Inspector O'Yee is also out with your husband.'

'Oh,' Mrs Feiffer said. She sounded very alone and lonely. 'Um, is Inspector Auden there?'

'He is also out. There is no one here but myself. I am sorry, Mrs Feiffer.'

There was another pause. Minnie said quickly, 'It is nothing to worry about.'

The line was silent. Minnie said, 'Mrs Feiffer? Are you still there?'

'Yes.' Minnie had a picture of her touching her hand to her face. She had a picture of Mrs Feiffer's eyes. 'Yes,' Mrs Feiffer said again, 'you can't break the rules about—you can't say where he is because it's against the rules.' There was no malice in her voice. It was a fact she accepted. She said, 'I understand.'

'Perhaps if you telephone a little later he will be here—'

'Yes. Yes, I'll do that. I'm sorry I—I'm very sorry I bothered you—'

'It is no bother.'

'Yes. Thank you.' Mrs Feiffer knew what it meant when more than two detectives were sent out together at four o'clock in the morning. She said, 'Yes—'

There was another pause.

'Mrs Feiffer—'

'Yes,' Mrs Feiffer's voice said. 'Yes. It's—it's all right. I—I just couldn't sleep, that was all. Um—goodnight, Minnie, and thank you.'

'Goodnight,' Minnie Oh said.

The line went dead.

In their apartment, Nicola Feiffer put her hand to her mouth. She looked at the open window in her bedroom. In the absence of a breeze, the curtains were very still.

The night was so dark.

The gangsters' plan was this: two of them, Crushed Toes and an eastern-end parked car gangster named The Shot In The Back Of The Head, would go back down to the third floor and begin working downwards room by room. The

Chopper Man would take the fire escape through the window of the third room and move carefully up to the roof. The Club (With Nails) would move up to the fifth floor and check the rooms there. If nothing was found, they would retrace their routes, the men on the roof and the fifth floor down towards the ground floor, and the two on the ground floor up towards the roof.

The detectives' plan was to send one man up the fire escape to cover the roof while the others entered the building through its main and only entrance. On the ground floor the uniformed officers would cover O'Yee and Feiffer from the stairs while the third man, Auden, covered them in the corridor. In that manner, with safety in numbers, they would work their way up to the roof and effectively search the entire building.

They were both good plans, each concocted independently of the other, but it was inevitable that on about the third floor, without a possibility in the universe of avoiding it, the two groups of belligerents, each searching for a third belligerent, would run head-on into each other.

Feiffer went over his plan for a second time. He said, 'If we run into the gangsters along the way I want them arrested, disarmed, and handcuffed to the nearest railing.' He said to Sun and Lee, 'Is that clear?'

Sun and Lee looked at him. Their heads moved imperceptibly in the most unclear of nodding agreements.

Feiffer looked at Spencer. This was, as far as Feiffer knew, his first piece of armed violence—he was still an unknown quantity. Feiffer asked him, 'All clear, Bill? Anything you want to ask?'

Auden waited with the contemptuous carelessness of a man who owned a Colt Python. Auden said to Spencer, 'It's all fairly straightforward.'

Spencer shrugged. He put a suggestion forward hesitantly. He said, 'Don't you think this is more in the Riot Squad's line, Inspector? After all, they're trained for this sort of thing.'

'It isn't a riot!' Auden told him. It was ridiculous. 'It's just a simple gunfight with a few gangsters!'

'It isn't a gunfight either,' Feiffer said. He didn't want those bullets from Auden's gun tearing holes in anything that moved. He said to Spencer, 'The Riot Squad are already committed to the water thing. This is our problem. I wouldn't feel justified calling them in.' He added, with a trace of annoyance at people who kept putting up the damned Riot Squad as the saviours of the northern hemisphere, 'We can handle it quite well enough by ourselves.'

'Yes, sir,' Bill Spencer said. 'It was just a suggestion.'

'You take the fire escape,' Feiffer told him. 'All you have to do is keep a watch that no one comes out of a window and tries to get on to the roof. I don't think anyone will. We'll meet you on the roof.'

Spencer began to say something. He changed his mind. He said, 'Yes, sir.'

'O.K.,' Feiffer said, 'Then let's get on with it.'

They all drew their pistols and went quickly across the road towards the entrance to the building.

'Around the back,' Feiffer ordered Spencer, and Spencer disappeared down the dark alley at the side of the building towards the fire escape.

At twenty-three minutes past four in the morning, they entered the building to do battle.

In the cells in Yellowthread Street, Mr Skilbeck and the Negro were discussing police brutality with Chen and The Fourth Gangster.

Since Chen spoke not a word of English and Mr Skilbeck and the Negro spoke only American, and The Fourth Gangster did nothing but groan, it was very much a one-way conversation.

They were each in separate cells, but if they leaned against the barred doors they could see each other.

The Negro said to Mr Skilbeck, 'Fucking cops.'

Mr Skilbeck nursed a bruise on the back of his neck where someone had hit him. He said, 'Yeah!'

'Fucking cops,' the Negro said.

'That's right,' Mr Skilbeck said. He leaned out and called to Chen, 'That's right all right, isn't it?'

Chen did not speak. The Fourth Gangster groaned.

'He doesn't talk English,' the Negro said. 'They probably scared the crap out of him.'

'Poor bastard,' Mr Skilbeck said. 'What could an old guy like him have done?'

'What did *I* do?' the Negro called back, 'It was just a joke—what did I do?'

'Right,' Mr Skilbeck said. He couldn't have agreed more. 'I've got a wife who's probably half out of her skull with worry. And they lock me up in here. What am I supposed to have done? You tell me that. They broke the other one's leg.'

'Right!' the Negro said. It was a conversation between a congregation of the converted. 'Right!' the Negro said. He shouted at the top of his lungs, 'Hey, you! I want my lawyer!' The steps leading up from the detention cells to the Station were empty of life. He shouted, 'I know my rights! I want a lawyer from the Navy brought down here!'

'Right,' Mr Skilbeck said. He yelled at the steps, 'Hey! We're American citizens and you can't keep us locked up!'

The Negro kicked at the bars of his cell door. They made a loud ringing sound. He kicked them again. The Negro yelled, 'Hey!'

'Hey!' Mr Skilbeck yelled.

'Hey!'

'Hey!'

'You up there!'

'Hey! Hey!'

'Hey, you people up there! Hey-hey-hey, you people!'

'Hey!' they yelled in unison.

'HEY-HEY-HEY—*HEY*!'

'Keep quiet,' Minnie Oh said. They saw her come down the stairs. She wasn't much.

'Hey,' the Negro said, 'get that Chink cop who arrested me!'

'He's not here,' Minnie Oh said. She glanced at Chen. Chen stood against the bars and looked at her wistfully. She said to the Negro, 'Shouting is a waste of time.'

'I want to get out,' Mr Skilbeck said, 'you can't keep me here. My wife—'

'Your wife knows you are here,' Minnie Oh said. 'You will both appear in Court in the morning.'

'What about him?' the Negro demanded. He meant Chen. 'What about him? He's got no rights, right? Poor old guy. What's he done? Did you beat him up too? What's he done?' He demanded, 'Get me the pig in charge. I want a lawyer right now.'

'In the morning,' Minnie Oh said. She turned to go.

'What's he done?' the Negro demanded, 'Hey? The old guy? What have you conned him into thinking he's done?' He said to Skilbeck, 'Right?'

'Right!' Mr Skilbeck said. 'Get me the chief cop!'

Minnie thought of Mrs Feiffer awake by the telephone. She said, 'There is nobody else here.'

'I'll bet!' Mr Skilbeck said. He felt very aggressive and deprived of his constitutional rights. He felt like Captain Dreyfus wrongly imprisoned on Devil's Island. He said, 'Yeah! What are we supposed to be guilty of?' He turned his head to the silent Chen. He said, 'What's that poor old guy supposed to have done if we're all hardened criminal types in here? You tell me that? Hey? Tell me that!'

Against all the regulations, Minnie told him.

The Mongolian was in a room on the fifth floor. He heard The Chopper Man clang stealthily up the metal rungs of the fire escape. He waited by the window to yank him in, but The Chopper Man was already on his way to the roof. His footsteps stopped clanging on the metal rungs as he stepped off on to the roof.

The Mongolian rubbed his fingers into his palms and listened for the others.

The Club (With Nails) was on the landing of the fifth floor. He touched the points of nails driven through the end of his wooden club and moved to the first door. The Mongolian heard the door squeak as The Club (With Nails) pushed it gently open. The Mongolian heard the floor of the first room squeak as The Club (With Nails) went across it. The Mongolian heard The Club (With Nails) open a cupboard or a closet in the room and then close it quietly again. The Mongolian went out into the corridor.

The Mongolian peered carefully over the corridor railing. He saw a group of people on the ground floor looking down at the body of the gangster who had gone down from the fourth floor with bits of the splintered railing. Two of the group were uniformed constables. The Mongolian saw Crushed Toes and The Shot In The Back Of The Head moving on the stairs at the third floor. They glanced at each other and then went quietly out of sight into the corridor. The Mongolian moved silently on the balls of his feet and stood to one side of the doorway to the first room. The Club (With Nails) came out of the first room looking down the corridor and did not see the Mongolian. He went into the second room. The Mongolian moved to one side of the door to the second room and waited.

On the third floor, as the cops came up to the first floor, Crushed Toes and The Shot In The Back Of The Head went into the first door.

Sun and Lee took up their positions on the stair landing of the first floor.

Feiffer said softly, 'Christopher—' and he and O'Yee went towards the first door on the first floor. The door hung open and light from a naked bulb swinging on a length of flex spilled out into the gloomy corridor. Auden came down behind them and stood at combat range against the railing.

O'Yee and Feiffer went into the first room. Auden cocked his revolver. Constable Sun took his revolver in two hands and drew a bead on the first door. Constable Lee rested his weapon on the stairhead and cocked it.

Feiffer and O'Yee came out. They shook their heads. They moved down the corridor towards the second room. O'Yee's hands were clammy with perspiration. He wiped them, one after the other, on his trouser leg and took a firmer grip on the revolver. He and Feiffer went into the second room.

On the roof, The Chopper Man took up position behind the tipped over plywood table the Mah-Jong players had deserted. A broken neon sign a street away intermittently flash-lit the roof every two or three seconds, but it was not a good light.

On the fire escape, Spencer was between two buildings and there was no light at all. Most of the windows to the rooms had muslin curtains pulled or newspaper pages stuck across them. He went as quietly as he could up the ringing metal rungs. He was at the fourth floor. He paused, listened, but there were no sounds. He heard his own breathing. He stopped to get control of it.

The Shot In The Back Of The Head on the third floor shook his head at the end of the corridor. No more rooms. Crushed Toes nodded. He jerked his head back to the landing. The Shot In The Back Of The Head nodded. They moved towards the landing to the stairs to the second floor.

'Nothing,' O'Yee said.

Feiffer nodded. He glanced at Auden and then, further back, at the two constables. He shook his head to signify that so far they had drawn a blank.

'Going up,' O'Yee said like a hoarse lift-driver with laryngitis.

Feiffer nodded. He and O'Yee and Auden went back down the corridor to the stairs.

'*Commandos Strike At Dawn*,' O'Yee tried softly. He

couldn't remember whether the Commandos in the film had all been killed or not.

'Shut up—' Feiffer hissed. They went excruciatingly quietly and carefully up the stairs to the second floor.

The Chopper Man heard someone coming up the fire escape. The Chopper Man drew himself further back behind the psychological cover of the plywood table and fingered his chopper.

The neon sign a street away went flash-pause-pause-flash-pause-flash-flash-pause—

Crushed Toes went into the second room on the second floor. He pointed to The Shot In The Back Of The Head to wait by the side of the door to give him cover. The Shot In The Back Of The Head nodded. He crouched against the wall and gave his full attention to the sounds from the second room. There was the creaking of Crushed Toes' shoes on the floor as he moved carefully. The Shot In The Back Of The Head craned his attention to the unseen interior of the second room.

The Chopper Man began counting the infinitely careful climbing steps of the man coming up the fire escape to the roof.

The Club (With Nails) crept out of the second room on the fifth floor and went along the corridor into the third and last room. He did not see the Mongolian. The Mongolian's eyes glittered and watched him go. Then the Mongolian padded silently to one side of the third room.

The cops stopped. Constable Sun glanced at Constable Lee and froze. O'Yee saw him too. Then Feiffer and then Auden. It was The Shot In The Back Of The Head. He had his back to them. He stood in the corridor with his back to them listening for something. Constable Sun started to move forward. He looked at Feiffer for approval. Feiffer nodded. Constable Lee asked silently for the same privilege. Feiffer flicked his finger at him to go. Constable Lee and Constable

Sun went noiselessly down the corridor towards The Shot In The Back Of The Head.

The Chopper Man counted the footsteps. They were ever so minutely louder. He thought it was the Mongolian. He was coming closer. The Chopper Man tapped his fingers against his chopper in anticipation. The sign went flash-pause-flash-pause-flash—

Crushed Toes moved through the darkened room soundlessly. His eyes pierced the shadows. He listened for the breathing of someone hiding.

In the corridor, The Shot In The Back Of The Head heard nothing. He felt something cold and hard go into his neck and he knew it was a gun. His mind stopped. He thought of his wife and children and forgot he wasn't married. It was the Mongolian. His mind stopped.

A whisper said, 'Gun.' It wasn't the Mongolian. The Shot In The Back Of The Head didn't know whose the voice was. He didn't know whether the voice was telling him it was a gun in his neck or whether the voice wanted him to hand his own gun over. He handed his own gun over. A hand took it. Another hand held him by the collar and drew him backwards. Another hand held another gun against his right ear.

'Back,' the voice of the neck gun said.

The Shot In The Back Of The Head went back.

It was the cops. On the landing, there were five cops. The five cops had five guns. The Shot In The Back Of The Head's mouth fell open. His mind could not take having five guns pointed at it. Five was too many. His mouth fell open.

'Mongolian,' a cop wearing a stained white suit said, 'Where?'

The Shot In The Back Of The Head's mouth stayed open.

Constable Lee rammed his gun barrel into it. He too said, 'Where?'

The Shot In The Back Of The Head tried to swallow. It was difficult. He said, 'Ahh-rumm—'

Constable Lee took his gun out of The Shot In The Back Of The Head's mouth.

'In there?' the stained suit cop said.

The Shot In The Back Of The Head shook his head. He felt his dentures rattle.

'Who?' the mouth cop said. He brought the gun up for another tonsils job, 'Who?'

'Crushed Toes.' The Shot In The Back Of The Head smiled to show how helpful he was. It didn't come out as a smile. The mouth gun cop moved back a little from him in case he was going to vomit. The Shot In The Back Of The Head said, 'Crushed Toes. Revolver. Second room. Mongolian. Looking for. I give up. Don't shoot,' and then he vomited.

Constable Lee handcuffed him to the railing. He said, 'Stay there.'

The Shot In The Back Of The Head nodded enthusiastically. The mouth gun cop gave him one more look at the mouth gun. The Shot In The Back Of The Head kept nodding.

Feiffer and O'Yee went down the corridor to the second room. Auden stayed a little way down the corridor outside the first room to cover them. Feiffer drew a breath. He heard someone moving in the unlit room. He tapped himself on the lapel with his thumb to signify that he would go in first. O'Yee did not argue. Feiffer saw a look of relief tinged with regret that his friend Feiffer was about to be killed cross O'Yee's Chinese-Irish face. Feiffer's confidence evaporated. He wiped his gun hand against the front of his coat, settled the weapon in his hand, and went in.

The Chopper Man saw the outline of a figure move on to the roof from the fire escape. He raised his gun and waited for the broken light to flash.

The Club (With Nails) came out of the third room on the fifth floor. He was looking down the corridor to a blank wall. The Mongolian stood poised behind him. The Club (With Nails) began to turn around.

The silhouette of the figure came directly into the Chopper

Man's line of fire. The Chopper Man's fingers started to take up the pressure on the trigger.

Feiffer said, 'Police!' and Crushed Toes opened fire. The room was pitch black. Feiffer saw something move against the window. He shot it. The figure said, 'Oh!' and the shooting stopped.

The Club (With Nails) jumped. The Mongolian's fist came down like a poleaxe and smashed his collarbone. The Club (With Nails) shouted, 'He's up here!' and Spencer on the roof dived for the ground as a spray of red-hot machine gun bullets passed over his head.

The Chopper Man said, 'Cop!' and lunged for the cover of the table. Spencer sheltered behind a pot-bellied stove that formed part of someone's alfresco kitchen and tried to locate the Chopper Man.

O'Yee wrenched Crushed Toes out of the room and kicked his pistol down two flights of stairs. Crushed Toes said, 'Oh—!' and tried to staunch the blood from the hole in his leg with his hand. His progress left a trail of blood as he went bodily to the landing. Feiffer stood outside the door to the second room and wondered where the bullets had gone. He looked behind him to part of the wooden railing that had two jagged holes in it. He swallowed.

At the landing, O'Yee took his handcuffs from his belt and manacled the bleeding Crushed Toes next to The Shot In The Back Of The Head. He undid the buckle of Crushed Toes' belt and pulled it out through his trouser loops. The blood seeped through Crushed Toes' pants and got on the stairs.

O'Yee tossed the belt to The Shot In The Back Of The Head. 'Do you know how to make a tourniquet?'

The Shot In The Back Of The Head gazed at him blankly.

'Show him,' O'Yee ordered Crushed Toes. He said to The Shot In The Back Of The Head, 'Watch and learn. You're in charge of the bleeding leg detail. If he dies I'll have you charged with murder.' He said to Feiffer and Auden, 'Did you hear?'

'Somewhere upstairs,' Auden said.

Lee said, 'Fifth floor.'

The five of them went up the stairs towards the fifth floor.

At the fourth floor, Feiffer's mind began to work again. He said, out of breath, 'I thought for a moment I'd killed him.'

'Bad luck,' Auden said. He kept waving that enormous gun of his. O'Yee said, 'Don't talk crap, Auden!'

They made it to the fifth floor. The Club (With Nails) was there. He was dead.

The neon sign finally broke or repaired itself and shone a steady wan light across the roof. Spencer peered out from behind the stove. There was no one. He listened. Nothing. The Chopper Man was behind the table. He had pulled a blanket over himself and he lay very still. He had almost chopped a cop. He fitted a new magazine into the Thompson and inched his fingers forward to work the cocking handle.

'I don't see it,' Feiffer said. There was only the broken body of The Club (With Nails) and the club itself on the corridor floor. The Mongolian was nowhere to be seen.

'What?' O'Yee asked. His eyes flickered towards the second and third rooms where Sun and Lee were.

'Didn't you hear it?'

'Hear what?'

'A bloody machine gun!'

'No. I heard your man shooting and then you shoot and someone get the axe up here. That's all.'

'I heard a machine gun.'

Constable Lee and Constable Sun came out of the second and third rooms simultaneously. They had found nothing. The Mongolian had gone.

Feiffer said, 'Where's Spencer?'

'Roof,' Auden said.

Feiffer looked at him. He *had* heard a machine gun. He knew a machine gun when he heard one. He said, 'The roof!'

Constable Lee said, 'One of the windows to the fire escape

was open. There was nobody on it.' He said, 'He must be on the roof.'

They went as one to the stairs to the roof. They found the inside door to the roof locked. They kicked it down. On the roof was the Mongolian.

The Mongolian was the biggest anything any of them had ever seen. He was over six foot three inches tall and he must have weighed well over two hundred and fifty pounds (two hundred and eighty-five). He stood in the middle of the roof and he looked at them. He looked at their guns. He looked at the constables' uniforms. He looked at Spencer's gun trained on him.

Spencer said, 'I've got him. He came up from the fire escape. He just appeared out of nowhere. And I've got him.'

The Mongolian looked at Spencer and he laughed.

'Holy Mother of God!' O'Yee said, 'you got him.'

Constable Sun and Constable Lee drew back a little. They knew Mongolians. They drew back.

'He's under arrest,' Spencer said, and the Mongolian began to come towards him. Spencer said to the Mongolian, 'You're under arrest.'

The Chopper Man tried to draw back the cocking handle of his chopper. It wouldn't move. There was a cartridge jammed in the breech. He worked to clear it.

'Don't move,' Spencer said to the Mongolian. The Mongolian stopped. He smiled at Spencer.

'Handcuffs,' Feiffer ordered Auden. Auden didn't look happy. He said to Spencer, 'Why didn't you shoot him?'

'Handcuffs,' Feiffer ordered Auden.

'He was unarmed,' Spencer said to Auden authoritatively. 'Police officers don't shoot unarmed men.'

'Handcuffs!' Feiffer said again.

Auden said, 'He's Spencer's prisoner, not mine. He's got his own bloody handcuffs.' He holstered his pistol.

'Do what you're told!' Feiffer ordered. He and O'Yee put

their own guns back. He said to Auden, 'Don't you argue the toss with me.'

The two constables put their guns away too. They looked at the Mongolian the way anglers look at a dead fighting fish. He *had* been a big one all right.

Auden pouted and drew his handcuffs. He glanced at Spencer unhappily and went to do his little part in Spencer's big glory. He said to Spencer, 'Beginner's luck,' and then the Mongolian caught hold of him and threw him at Spencer. The Mongolian charged. He caught Constable Lee on the bridge of his nose with his fist-hammer and broke the septum. Constable Lee fell against Constable Sun and the Mongolian kicked Constable Sun in the groin.

Feiffer grabbed for his pistol. The Mongolian caught his hand and crushed it. The gun came out of its own accord and clattered on to the roof. O'Yee reached for it and the Mongolian stamped on his hand with his boot and dislocated three of O'Yee's fingers. Auden was back on his feet. He had the Python out. He thought, 'Now, you bastard!' and levelled the gun at the Mongolian's back a fraction before the Mongolian turned and kicked him against the upturned plywood Mah-Jong table. The Python crashed against the side of Spencer's head and he only vaguely saw someone stand up from behind the table with something in his hands.

Feiffer saw the machine gun. His hand was useless. He tried to pick up his revolver with his left hand. He dropped it. He saw the machine gun and shouted, 'Get down! Get down!' He tried to get the gun with both hands.

The Thompson's mechanism would not work. The Chopper Man was wrenching at it to clear the action. He swung the muzzle towards Feiffer and O'Yee and the two uniformed men. A single shot went off and cleared the mechanism. The bullet smashed into the pot-bellied stove and whanged off over the roof. He pointed the muzzle of the machine gun at the Mongolian. Spencer had Auden's Python in his hand. Feiffer shot The Chopper Man between the eyes and The Chopper

Man staggered to the edge of the roof and went over. Feiffer's smashed hand dropped the revolver.

The Mongolian's eyes turned themselves on to Spencer. The Mongolian drew his kukri. Spencer aimed the Python at the Mongolian. The Mongolian came forward. Spencer pulled the trigger. The regulation .38 calibre bullet went into the Mongolian's mass of flesh and disappeared. The Mongolian came forward. Spencer pulled the trigger a second time. The gun kicked high in his hand and there was an explosion that echoed across the roofs. The Mongolian started going backwards. He moved the kukri in a funny arc and Spencer shot him again.

The Mongolian fell dead.

Spencer looked at the dead Mongolian. He went to help Auden to his feet. Auden said, 'Thanks,' and looked at the dead Mongolian.

'I've never shot anyone before,' Spencer said. He saw Feiffer and O'Yee helping the constable with the broken nose. He said to Auden, 'Really. I've never done anything like this before.' He looked at the big gun in his hand. He said, trying to make up for something, 'I suppose something like this must have cost a fortune.'

Auden looked at the Python. He looked at Spencer. He looked at the dead Mongolian and he looked at the Python again.

He said, 'Keep it,' and went to join the casualty group.

Spencer thought, 'I always thought if I had to shoot anyone I'd be sick, or I'd break down and cry.' He waited. It was odd. He didn't do either.

It was Minnie Oh ringing from the Station. Nicola Feiffer said, 'Yes?'

'They're all right,' Minnie Oh said. 'There was some trouble, but they're all all right.' She said, 'Constable Cho was killed.'

'I'm sorry.'

'Inspector Feiffer is all right. He's hurt his hand, but it's only a minor injury. He should be home in a few hours. There's nothing for you to worry about.'

There was a pause.

Minnie Oh said, 'I thought you'd like to know.'

'Yes.'

'He'll be home in a few hours,' Minnie Oh said. 'There's nothing to worry about.'

'Thank you,' Mrs Feiffer said, 'it was kind of you to—'

'I have to go now.'

'Of course,' Mrs Feiffer said. 'Thank you for telling me.'

'Goodnight,' Minnie Oh said.

'Thank you,' Mrs Feiffer said. She put the receiver down very gently. It only made a very slight click at Minnie's end of the line.

Minnie looked at the Station clock. It was almost morning. She thought it would be nice to have someone to go home to.

'There'll be riots today,' Sister Sung said. The victims of the Camphorwood Lane battle occupied all the casualty treatment rooms. She finished tying a neat bow in the wrist sling at the back of Feiffer's neck and looked at the X-Ray pictures of the fractured right-hand carpus and metacarpus bones. She said, 'It'll be back to normal in a month or two.' She said, 'We'll have a busy day here tomorrow with the riots.'

'They'll turn the water on again in forty-eight hours,' Feiffer consoled her. He said, 'They always do.'

'It's a great pity,' Sister Sung said. 'Why do the Communists cause so much trouble?'

'They're not the only ones,' Feiffer said. His fingers hurt.

'Do you like being a policeman?' Sister Sung asked pleasantly. She checked the bow she had made and thought it was quite neat.

'Yes.'

She smiled at him. She said, 'I think you're a very good policeman. We all do.'

'Thank you,' Feiffer said. His fingers were very painful.

'Yes,' Sister Sung said. She smiled at him for the second time in as many seconds. She said, 'Do you think you could possibly do something about our wheelchair, Inspector Feiffer?' She said, 'Perhaps on your way home?'

Feiffer's fingers hurt like hell.